CHEER FOR THE DEAD

Also by ELI COLTER

THE GULL COVE MURDERS

CHEER FOR THE DEAD

A Pat Campbell Detective Story

by ELI COLTER

WILDSIDE PRESS

1

THE LATE MORNING SUN, slanting in through the broad office window which faced the street, cast the shadow of Patrick Campbell's bent head across the black ledger spread open on his desk. In the black ledger he kept data on past cases for future reference. In the red ledger lying beside the black one he jotted data on current cases. The drone of downtown Los Angeles traffic came in through the open window, but he didn't hear it. His thoughts were far away, and he was writing slowly in the black ledger:

Wednesday, July 10, 1946. I see by the morning paper that Wark Andross is dead: dead, cremated, ashes scattered. And I never discovered any trace of his daughter Mary. I wish he could have seen her once again before he died. Well, she moves into the red ledger today. I *have* to find her now.

The detective closed the black ledger and replaced his desk pen in its onyx holder. He sat erect, pushed back his chair and got to his feet. There was an amused light in his hazel eyes, as he walked into the outer office and paused by the desk, where his assistant, Rick Eilers, sat poring over a racing form.

Eilers, blond, blue-eyed, and half a head shorter than Campbell, looked up inquiringly.

Campbell sat down on the edge of Eilers' desk: his massive

1

shoulders sagged a little, there was a slight air of weariness about his entire big frame. He said, "I was just re-reading the account of Wark Andross' obsequies, Rick. He was young to die; only ten years older than I."

Eilers shoved aside the racing form. "That makes him fifty-two when he died. You'd known him a long time, hadn't you?"

"Twenty years, kid. And we've been pretty close to each other ever since he came to L.A." Campbell raised a hand to smooth back his thick, sandy hair. "I liked him better than any other man I ever knew. When I first met him he'd been married to his lovely blond wife three years, and his daughter, Naomi, was about a year old."

"That's when you were living in Seattle, of course; and Andross was living there too, then. He left Seattle and came to L.A. in 1938—when his wife died—isn't that what you told me? And he really made all his pile of dough, and built up his big reputation as a financier, after he came to California?"

Campbell nodded. "That's right. What I mean, he really made a pile, too. Must have left between five and six million."

"Quite a sock full." Eilers grinned. "And no kids to inherit but Naomi. I'll have to get acquainted with the gal."

Campbell said, "Naomi *isn't* the only heir. Wark had another daughter by a former marriage, six years older than Naomi. When Wark first came to L.A. he looked me up immediately, and asked me to find his older daughter Mary. I've been looking for her ever since, and never ran across the least trace of her."

"You've been holding out on me," Eilers accused.

"No I haven't, Rick. Wark asked me not to mention it to anyone, even you. Finding Mary had become an obsession with him; he hadn't seen her since she was seven years old.

All he ever knew was that his former wife left Seattle with the child and came to L.A. I think that's why he came here himself. He hoped Mary was still here."

Eilers said, "And what does this all boil down to?"

Campbell slid off the desk. "I have to find that girl, that's what—before Wark's will is read. I owe it to him. He paid me a lot of money for time I used, for effort expended that brought him no return. I can't quit on him now!"

Eilers looked dubious. "How the hell are you going to find her now, if you haven't been able to get a line on her in all these years?"

Campbell said, "That's your question—you answer it. I'm going out to lunch. If anybody comes in while I'm gone, I'll be back in less than an hour."

He took his hat off the rack by the door and went out of the office suite, leaving Eilers gazing speculatively after him.

Eilers muttered, "Anybody else would be stuck! By comparison a needle in a haystack would be duck soup."

The big detective did not go directly to a restaurant. He went, instead, down the street to another office building on the next corner beside which there were three green benches to accommodate people waiting for buses. There, with the roar of Los Angeles traffic in his ears blotting out every other sound, he sat down on one of the benches to do a little thinking and figuring.

He was thinking of Wark Andross, the lonely disappointed man he had known and liked for so long. There could, he thought, be any number of answers to his failure to find Mary Andross. Mary's mother could have married again, the child could have grown up under her stepfather's name. "Or, the woman could have deliberately taken another name to prevent

Wark's finding her," he told himself. "It isn't hard to drop out of sight in a town as big as L.A., when you don't want to be found."

He frowned, thinking that Wark's assignment had been a difficult one. There were no pictures of the woman and the child Mary, not even a kodak snapshot. Wark had said that Naomi's mother, Sharon, wouldn't have had them about the house. Sharon had been a beauty when she was young, and Naomi had grown up to look just like her. The first wife, Mary's mother, had been plain. Proud as hell, Wark had said. Campbell thought this had been one of the oldest triangles known to man. Wark, a handsome devil himself, married to a plain woman, falling in love with a beauty, and divorcing the plain one to marry the beauty.

Campbell sighed impatiently, rose from the bench, and started down the street toward the restaurant where he habitually lunched. "And," he told himself, "after he was married to the beauty, he found out where he was wrong." He found out he'd been happier with the first wife who had loved him and waited on him willingly. Life hadn't been very pleasant with Sharon, spoiled and demanding, who expected to be pampered every hour of the day and cared less for a man than the money he made. And the first wife had been so hurt and bitter over being discarded for the beauty, she had never wanted to see him or have anything to do with him again. Poor devil, Campbell thought. He certainly messed things up for himself.

As he neared the restaurant, his mind went on to the will Wark had left. Wark's lawyer, Drake Freedon, had it in his safe. Campbell felt again the sense of shock that had struck at him when he had opened the morning *Times* and seen that meager article concerning Wark's death. Wark himself had given the detective a sketchy account of the will; some smaller bequests, but the bulk of his fortune to be divided between his two daughters. The will was to be read a week from the day of Wark's burial, the cremation and ash-scattering in this case—if one could call that a burial.

The big detective was frowning heavily as he turned in the doorway and found his way to his favorite table. He'd relay all this to Eilers later, after he'd thought it through himself. Eilers had hit the troublesome point when he had asked how Pat hoped to find Mary now, when all the years of search had failed. The biggest hope was the ads he'd run so often in the personal columns, Campbell thought. That was his most likely avenue now. If Wark's first wife ever read the papers thoroughly, she couldn't help knowing that Patrick Campbell, offices in the McClintock Building, wanted to get in touch with her.

"And there's a long chance," Campbell told himself as he settled in his chair and picked up the menu card, "there's a really fair chance that now, since his death, she might figure there was some hope of her being mentioned in the will, and look me up. Or send the girl to me."

He ordered beer and sandwiches, leaned back in his chair and looked around the crowded room. He saw two or three people he knew, nodded and smiled silent greeting, then his gaze caught on a man just making his way to the cash register to pay his bill.

The man's back was toward him, but there was something familiar in that back and head. Also, there was something a little incongruous about seeing the man here, as if the fellow shouldn't be here. But he did not for the instant follow through the association, or understand why he had that immediate impression.

Then the man turned, as he paid his check and went on toward the restaurant door, and the detective saw that it was Ransome, who had for a long time been Wark Andross' head gardener. And he knew why he had the feeling of seeing someone who shouldn't be here at this time of day. This wasn't Ransome's day off. He should be on the job at the Andross place at Beverly Hills. Ransome didn't come all the way in to Los Angeles for his noon luncheon; he brought it with him from home, or he ate there with the Andross staff of servants. What little Campbell could see of Ransome's face looked dour and worried.

On sudden impulse, the detective left his table and went quickly to the doorway, but Ransome had disappeared in the crowd thronging the street. Campbell went slowly back to his table, frowning again. He had an unshakable impression that the gardener's being here at this time stemmed from something radically wrong. He decided to get through with his lunch quickly, hurry back to the office and do a little telephoning, unless some other lead turned up.

As he ate, his mind kept dwelling on the task of finding Mary Andross, and the recurring hope stayed with him that the girl's mother would have noticed the personals, might even had cut one out and tucked it away for future reference, might now come to his office in answer to the ad's summons, or send Mary to him. Even though she had been so wounded at Wark's deserting her for a beautiful woman that she had refused to accept the least aid from him while he lived, a lot of years had passed since then. Mary was a grown woman now, twenty-eight her next birthday, if he remembered correctly. Mary herself might have something to say about her probable inheritance.

It was the soundest hope he had right now, anyway. The

detective finished his light lunch, paid his check and went out of the restaurant. He went slowly along the street, wondering if there was any chance that he might get another glimpse of Ransome. He'd like to know why the gardener wasn't at the Andross place in Beverly Hills. But there was no further sight of Ransome anywhere.

2

WHEN CAMPBELL RETURNED FROM the restaurant, the door to his inner office was closed, and Eilers told him he had company. "A young lady by the name of Bess Holloway."

Campbell said thanks, hung up his hat, and went on into his office. He thought for an instant Eilers was kidding him, that it was a child sitting in the clients' chair before his desk. Then she turned her face to look up at him, hearing his footsteps and the closing of the door, and he saw that she was a very small young woman whose age might be anything from twenty to thirty. Some instinct told him immediately who she was; he didn't believe in coincidence.

He went around behind his desk to his swivel chair, smiling across the desk at her as he sat down. "Miss Holloway? I'm Pat Campbell. My assistant said you wanted to see me."

The girl's plain, dark face lighted in an answering smile, her clear gray eyes widened in amazement. "You're the biggest man I ever saw!" she marveled. "Do you mind telling me how tall you are?"

Campbell chuckled. "Not in the least. I'm six feet and six inches tall, and I weigh two hundred and seventy pounds. And you're just about the littlest girl I ever saw to be grown up. Do you mind?"

She laughed delightedly, and he noticed that in her laughter she looked less plain. Some plain women do, when they smile. "Not in the least!" she assured him. "I'm four feet and ten inches tall and I weigh ninety pounds. But I'm plenty grown up. I'm twenty-seven years old." She sobered, and the laughter went out of her eyes. "I came to see you— Just a minute."

She opened the flat black pocketbook lying in her lap, and the detective's quick gaze scrutinized her closely while her attention was withdrawn from him. The plain little red felt hat on the back of her head had been cleaned more than once; it hadn't cost much in the first place. Her red dress was neat and smart, but it was not new and it hadn't cost a great deal, either. She took a folded paper from the black pocketbook, closed the purse and handed the paper to Campbell across the desk.

She said, "Two years ago my mother was stricken with double pneumonia. When she knew she wasn't going to get well, she gave me this paper, and said if ever that man died I was to bring it to you. I think maybe she would have explained what it was all about, but she was already so ill she could barely speak a few words. She said you would understand, and you would tell me what I was supposed to know. I saw the news of Wark Andross' death in the paper this morning, so I came right away. I hope those two clippings will mean more to you than they do to me."

Campbell unfolded the sheet of notepaper. Stuck to the paper by a couple of strips of transparent adhesive tape were two old clippings from the *Times*. One was merely a picture of Wark Andross. The caption underneath said that he had just put over another million-dollar deal. The other was Campbell's own advertisement, cut from the personal column.

Madam: when you got your divorce from W.A. and left Puget Sound with Mary, you left no trace. For your child's sake, it is imperative that we get in touch with you. Will you kindly communicate with Patrick Campbell, offices in the McClintock Bldg.?

The detective folded the paper with two fingers, and glanced up at the girl, who sat watching him, waiting for him to finish looking at the clippings.

She said anxiously, "Well? What has it got to do with me?"

Campbell studied her face for a moment, hesitating, then he said, "Haven't you, honestly, any idea? Can't you put two and two together, Miss Holloway?"

She shook her head, frowning a little. "Well, because of the picture, I suppose the W.A. in your advertisement means Wark Andross. And some woman divorced him, and went away from Puget Sound with a child named Mary, presumably Wark Andross' child. Of course, I'd figured that much out. And I'd thought maybe at some time Mother had known the woman and the child Mary, but if I ever saw them I don't remember it. And I still don't see what they could have to do with me, Mr. Campbell."

Campbell said, "Let's take it a little slower. In a minute I'll ask you a few questions, and maybe we can come to an understanding about this. But first, I want you to tell me a little bit about yourself—where you came from, where you live, where you work, and what you remember about your parents."

The girl asked, "Where's Puget Sound?"

"In the state of Washington. Seattle is the town where Andross lived when the divorce was granted. I'm waiting to hear about you."

The girl sat up straight in the clients' chair, her hands

clasped about the black pocketbook. "I don't remember coming from anyplace else; as far back as I can remember we've always lived in Los Angeles. Mother said I was born in San Francisco, and that we moved to Los Angeles when I was small, but I don't remember anything about it. I don't remember much about my father, either. He died when I was ten years old. What little I do remember is kind; he was always good to Mother and me, but he didn't make a great deal of money. We never got enough ahead to buy a home, we've never even lived in a house, just rooms and apartments. When I was old enough to go to work, I made Mother stay home and it was easier on her then. She was little, like me, and not very strong. During the war I worked in different defense plants, in the cafeterias. I've always worked in cafés and restaurants. It was the best I could get without experience. I never went to high school; I went to work the minute I finished grade school, so Mother could take it a little easier. But she failed fast. I guess that's about all. I still live in the rooms we had when Mother died. I work in a downtown café. This is my day off. That's why I could come to see you today."

Campbell said, "All very clearly stated. What was your father's full name?"

"Ethan Holloway, Ethan Roy Holloway."

"What's your first name?"

"Elizabeth. I haven't any middle name, Mr. Campbell. Just Elizabeth Holloway. Everybody calls me Bess."

Campbell said, "Then I'll call you Bess. It will make for less confusion." He paused for a moment, thinking, choosing words. "I'll try not to be blunt. I don't want you to be startled or upset, but I don't know any gentle way of saying what I have to tell you. Do you remember your mother's full name?"

"Oh, yes, of course. It was always the same, she never changed it; she married a man of the same name, you see. She just became Mrs. Holloway instead of Miss Holloway. Her full name was Elizabeth Anne Holloway. I was named for her."

Campbell said, "Suppose I tell you a little story. Maybe that'll be the easiest way. If it sounds a trifle like a fairy story, remember that I have legal documents to prove all I say. What's your birth date, Bess?"

"September the fifteenth," Bess answered promptly. "1918. I'll be twenty-eight next September."

"All right. Listen closely. Remember everything you've told me, and begin putting two and two together, now. Interrupt me if you feel you must, but I'll be able to tell it more quickly if you don't. When the United States entered the First World War in April, 1917, Wark Andross was twenty-three years old. He was in love with a girl named Elizabeth Anne Holloway, and he didn't want to go to war. He didn't enlist. He married his Elizabeth Anne, on the tenth of June, 1917. His number came up in the draft in February, 1918, and he went away to war, eventually to France."

Campbell paused, looking steadily at Bess. Her eyes were wide, and her small dark face had paled, but she asked no questions. The detective went on with his story.

"I don't know everything I should know about this, Bess. Wark was careful of what he told me, even though we'd been friends for a long time. I do know that Wark was always an extraordinarily handsome man and that Elizabeth Anne was a plain and quiet little thing. I think she must have loved him a great deal. On September the fifteenth in 1918, their daughter was born, and Wark's wife named the child Mary Elizabeth.

Then the war was over, the armistice was signed on November the eleventh, and Wark came home in December, shortly before Christmas. Wark's wife had made a friend while he was gone, a big handsome blond girl named Sharon. Wark fell head over heels in love with Sharon."

Campbell paused again.

Bess said, almost whispering, "It isn't a fairy story. It's a Greek tragedy."

"Yes, I'm afraid it's something like that, if we knew everything. When Mary Elizabeth was three years old, Elizabeth Anne divorced Wark Andross and he married Sharon. When Mary Elizabeth was seven years old, Elizabeth Anne took her and went away from Seattle, so quietly that Wark knew nothing about it for several months. She went with the child to Los Angeles. About the years in between, I know nothing. Wark kept that to himself. I only know that he made every effort to trace his ex-wife and his daughter, his older daughter, after Naomi Andross was born. When his wife died he came to Los Angeles, mainly in the hope of finding Elizabeth Anne and Mary again, I think. He came to me—I'd known him in Seattle —and put the search in my hands. I've been trying to find you and your mother ever since."

Bess said slowly, "You—you say you have legal documents to prove all this?"

"I have a copy of your mother's and father's wedding certificate, your birth certificate, and a copy of the divorce decree. Wark gave them to me when he asked me to undertake the search for you. I think your mother was so hurt that she never wanted to see him again. She did everything she could to prevent his ever tracing her, to push him out of your memory— telling you that you were born in San Francisco, teaching you to believe that your stepfather was your own father—though you couldn't have remembered Wark much, since you saw him only at intervals after you were three years old."

Bess said, "It's hard to grasp. It's hard to believe. Then—the Naomi Andross I've read about in the society news is my half-sister!"

"That's right. Though she may not know it. I doubt that she does. She is six years your junior. Your mother didn't want you to have anything to do with your father while she was living, or while he was living, that's plain from what she did. But I think she hoped he might leave something to you when he died. That's why she told you to come to me."

Bess' eyes brightened, and she caught her breath. "Oh! Did he? Even a couple of hundred dollars would make so much difference. Everything's so awfully high, now. We were always in debt; Mother was sick so much, we never got ahead of the doctor and drug bills. Then there was the funeral expense; it was the least I could do for her, I wanted her to have the best. I finally paid up the last bill only two months ago, and I was so happy to be out of debt. But if my father left me anything—it's so strange to think of Wark Andross as my father! —but if he left me anything, I'd be awfully grateful. Maybe I could get a better place to live, maybe even a whole house of my own out of town somewhere, when the housing shortage lets up a little."

Campbell smiled. "I don't think the housing shortage is going to bother you much, Bess. You never thought of marrying?"

Bess sighed, and her eyes darkened at the awakening of painful memory. "My boy friend was one of the first overseas. Mother didn't want us to marry until he came back. She said it wasn't easy for a woman left alone with a child to bring up.

I knew enough about that to believe her. He was killed in Germany two weeks before VE day. You mean—my father did leave me something, Mr. Campbell?"

"He certainly did. I don't know exactly what he was worth, around five or six million in cash, stocks and bonds, and he owned two homes, a big swank place in Beverly Hills, and the Canyon House. The Canyon House is in Flour Gold Canyon, in the Sierra Madre foothills out toward San Bernardino. Two hundred acres of land go with the house. Wark left Naomi half of the five or six million and the Beverly Hills place. He left you the other half of the money, and the Canyon House."

Bess sat staring at him, dumb with amazement, her hands gripping the black pocketbook so hard that the knuckles stood out. She said finally, incredulously, "He left all that to me?"

"That's right. But keep it to yourself for the present—until after the will is read. It's to be read one week from yesterday, which will be next Tuesday, July the sixteenth. The reading is to be done at the Canyon House, for some reason known only to Wark Andross. It's up to Drake Freedon, Wark's lawyer, to have everybody concerned on the spot. You are my only responsibility in that direction. I'll drive you out to the Canyon House in my car. I want you to do exactly as I tell you, Bess."

"Yes. Of course, I will. I hardly know what I'm saying. I feel light-headed. I don't know what I expected when I came here today, but it certainly never was anything like this. What am I to do?"

Campbell leaned forward, both arms on his desk. "I want you to go home and say nothing of this to anyone at all, not anyone! Give up your job at the restaurant. Just tell them you're quitting, they don't need to know why. I'll advance you five hundred dollars. Get yourself a good outfit of clothes;

I want you to go out to the Canyon House looking like Wark Andross' daughter. Then just stay home and take it easy, fill up on good food, get plenty of rest, and be feeling on top of the world next Tuesday. I'll come for you at nine o'clock in the morning. The will isn't to be read until one o'clock in the afternoon, but it will take a little while to get there, and I want plenty of time. We may run into trouble, Bess."

The girl started and her eyes widened in alarm. "Trouble? How?"

"I don't know. But think a minute: doesn't it seem odd to you that a man as influential and well-known as your father could be fatally hurt in an accident, could die in the hospital the same day, and not a word of it get into the papers until after he was buried? Even I didn't know a thing about it till I saw the *Times* this morning. Not even Drake Freedon knew: I called him up and talked to him after I read the paper. Some pretty drastic pressure was brought to bear for some reason, Bess."

"Yes. Yes, it looks like it. But—what does it mean?"

"I don't know; I'm not sure yet. But I do know Wark was afraid of something. I know from things he said to me the last time I saw him. I know from veiled hints he made, hints that he thought something was going to happen to him."

Bess said anxiously, "That doesn't sound—I don't like the sound of it. What are you trying to say?"

"I'm saying I don't believe it was any accident that killed Wark Andross, Bess. I think your father was murdered."

3

CAMPBELL SAT IN THE outer office talking with Rick Eilers. Bess Andross had been gone a little over half an hour. Campbell had taken down her address, and impressed it upon her to call him at any time she might have reason to. Then he had gone into Eilers' office to talk over his conversation with Bess.

"She certainly took it in her stride," Campbell finished his recital. "No near-hysterics, no extravagant protestations, no histrionics. I have an idea Bess is pretty much like Elizabeth Anne in character and temperament, as well as being almost a duplicate of her physically. If so, I can understand why Wark was so set on finding his first wife again. Naomi's mother was the type that wants the world on a lollipop stick with a golden fence around it, and runs to fat in the forties. So's Naomi."

Eilers made a wry face. "Exit Naomi, for Mrs. Eilers' son. Didn't I hear you talking to Hoolihan a while ago? Was Andross the subject of conversation?"

"Yes. Just doing a little spade work," Campbell answered. Lieutenant Hoolihan, of Los Angeles Homicide, had been Campbell's personal friend for years. "I didn't dig up much. Hoolihan didn't know a great deal to pass on. No inquest, no autopsy—no reason for either. Wark's money and influence were employed by Naomi to clamp a soft pedal on the press."

"Even to repressing the kind of accident and injuries that

took him off," Eilers said. "Hoolihan know anything about that?"

"No. But I already knew that much when I came down to the office this morning. I was reading the paper while I was eating breakfast. Got right up from the table and called Drake Freedon. He'd called the Andross family physician the minute he read the paper, and got the lowdown from the doc, which he passed on to me. You've been out to the Beverly Hills place with me a time or two. You remember the layout of the place in general, don't you?"

Eilers nodded, a picture in his mind of the white-plaster and red-tile buildings crowning a low truncated hill lavishly land-scaped from base to summit. "Some joint."

Campbell said, "You'll remember the swimming pools, the shallow one for youngsters and everybody, and the deep one for adults only. The water in the big pool was fifteen feet deep and no one was ever allowed in it but expert swimmers, and damn few of them; it was practically Wark's private pool. Wark could swim like a fish, and he liked to go out and paddle around in the deep pool by himself on moonlit nights. Apparently, he'd gone out for one of those moonlight swims; somehow the sluice gate had been lifted—and Wark dived from the high springboard, thinking he had fifteen feet of water waiting for him."

"Instead of about ten inches?"

"Right. Seven or eight inches, to be exact. Wark's personal man servant, Thibault, noticed the time, thought it was strange Wark hadn't come in, went looking for him, and found him on his back under the diving board in the water with his skull cracked like an egg shell. They rushed him to the hospital, but he died before midnight without regaining consciousness. Does it seem reasonable to you that, even at night and with none too bright a moon, Wark wouldn't have noticed from the springboard that the shine of the water was a damned sight farther below him than it should have been?"

"On the face of it, no; it doesn't seem reasonable. But a lot of people can be God-awful absent-minded, Pat; maybe Andross was. How about that steel-grille fence, six feet high if it's an inch, all the way around the pool to keep kids out, with sharp spikes on top to prevent them from climbing over it? Who has keys to the gate?"

"I wouldn't know, Rick. The gate's always locked, but I've no idea who'd have the keys or how many keys there were." Campbell paused for an instant, seeing the pool in his mind's eye, the steel fence, the wide tile walk completely surrounding the pool outside the fence, and the twenty-foot cypress windbreak outside the walk, shading and enclosing the fenced pool. "Anything could go on inside that cypress windbreak and remain completely cloaked from view of anybody in the house or on the grounds."

"Yes, I guess you're right there. It could So what?"

"So somebody could have lifted the sluice gate, drained the pool, lain in wait for Wark, slugged him on the head and pitched him in. I want to know how many people were familiar with his habit of swimming alone by moonlight. I want to know how many people carried a key to the grille gate, or had access to the key. If the sluice gate was lifted by accident, why didn't it stay up and drain the pool entirely? How did it happen to shut down again just in time to leave a deceptive glimmer of water covering the tile and concrete? How could anyone have been inside the grille fence and manipulated the lever controlling the sluice gate without realizing what he'd done?"

Eilers said, "Doesn't sound good, does it? Plenty of room

for suspicion. Still, Andross could have been wool-gathering and failed to note the water level in time. Maybe the rest of the water would have drained out if Thibault hadn't discovered Andross and shut the sluice gate—or do you know that he did not close it?"

"No. I don't know. He could have closed it either before or after he brought Wark up the pool ladder. Freedon wasn't too coherent about it. He'd been shocked out of a year's growth. The doctor was satisfied it was an accident; everybody seems to agree with him—but me."

"You tell Freedon you didn't believe in the accident theory?"

"No. I didn't tell Hoolihan either. I don't want it to get around that any suspicions have been raised in any quarter. Maybe if I give the murderer enough rope he'll hang himself."

Eilers said, "You're bound and determined to have it murder, aren't you?"

Campbell smiled thinly. "I know it was murder. If nobody else knew Wark well enough to realize that he couldn't have done such a fool thing, I do."

"So now we go on a still hunt for motive; question before the court—who could profit by your friend Wark Andross' death at this particular time?"

"Right. There can be a hell's mint of motives where five-six million bucks are concerned, kid."

Eilers said, "I'll buy that. I keep thinking about the way it was hushed up. I thought of it the first thing when I read the account in the *Times*—a little sketchily, I will admit. Nothing leaked at the hospital, no memorial service, no funeral, body cremated and ashes scattered at Andross' own request, all done with neatness and dispatch."

Campbell rose from the chair where he had been sitting by Eilers' desk. "I'll have to admit that much is true; Wark did request, and vehemently, that there be no funeral, no fuss, just a quiet cremation and ashes scattered, no flowers and no friends. Such a request always offers a perfect set-up for murder. Get up off your el fideldo and take on a little leg work, will you?"

"Right-o, boss! Where to?"

"Check up on Bess' story. I'm satisfied she's Mary Elizabeth Andross, haven't the least doubt of it. But we can't be too sure. Look up Elizabeth Anne's obituary. Call San Francisco and check on the possible birth of an Elizabeth Holloway, born September the fifteenth, 1918. Dig up L.A. vital statistics for a marriage license issued to Elizabeth Anne Andross and Ethan Roy Holloway, around 1925 to 1927. I've already been through 'em, but maybe I missed something because I didn't know what I was looking for."

"What were you looking for?"

"A license issued to Elizabeth Anne Andross and a man, of course. You clear those points, and we'll have all the proof we need in regard to Bess."

"I do all the hard work," Eilers mourned. "And how will you be spending your time while I'm dutifully sweating it out in the hot sun and stuffy, dusty files?"

"Not lapping up any long cool ones," Campbell said dryly. "I'm on my way to offer condolences to Naomi Andross, and to have a little chin on the side with Thibault—or anybody else who looks promising."

Eilers grinned. "You can't make any money that way—your client's dead. Or will you take it out of Naomi's hide?"

Campbell said, "You leave that to me. Get going. I'll see you later on in the day."

They went out of the offices together. Campbell turned toward the parking lot, and Eilers headed for the Hall of Records.

Campbell kept seeing Bess' small figure upright in the clients' chair, watching him and listening courteously. There was something about her, he told himself. She was one of those who didn't need beauty. Beauty fades, but what she had would only grow richer and more mellow through the years. It would be a lucky man who got Bess Andross.

When Campbell walked up to the portico-shaded front door, it swung open before he could touch the chime button, and the Andross butler, Grannat, stood there smiling a subdued welcome.

"Mr. Campbell, sir! It seems a long time since we've had the pleasure of your company. I wish we could be greeting you on a happier occasion, sir."

"I wish you could too, Grannat. It was a terrible shock to me. I wonder if Miss Naomi would feel like seeing me?"

"She is expecting you, sir. She saw you coming up the drive, and told me to bring you back to the sitting room."

Campbell followed the butler down the wide hall to the secluded retreat beyond the long drawing room. Naomi, lounging on a chaise longue, sat erect and swung her feet to the floor as Campbell came in. She was a big girl, full bodied, and tall; in other surroundings and in another day buxom would have been the word for Naomi Andross. Her hair was a clean light yellow. It would turn ash blond as she grew older if nature was allowed her way. But the genuine striking beauty of her face and her large blue eyes would temporarily blind any man to the possibility of future change, to—as Campbell had said—a tendency to run to fat in the forties.

She smiled up at the big detective and gestured him to a chair. "It's nice to see you, Pat. I wish Dad were here to greet you. He was always so fond of you."

"No more so than I was of him." Campbell took the chair she had indicated, and shifted it a little so that he sat facing her. Naomi sank back on the chaise longue. "I suppose this will postpone your wedding to Drake Freedon now."

Naomi said indifferently, "Oh, no; not if I really had any idea of marrying Drake, it wouldn't. Dad wouldn't want that. He always hated fuss of any kind, you know. It's just a rather flimsy excuse to put off indefinitely an alliance that never really appealed to me in the first place. It was Dad who wanted me to marry Drake. I didn't mind being engaged to Drake if it made Dad happy."

"I see. I didn't know that." Campbell looked past her, through the window that overlooked gardens and lawns and one end of the shallow swimming pool. "I haven't quite grasped it yet, that Wark's gone, so suddenly, so needlessly, through somebody's carelessness."

"Carelessness!" Naomi echoed blankly.

"Well, you don't think the sluice gate lifted itself do you, Naomi?"

Naomi's eyes turned a little hard, and her expression chilled. "See here, Pat, if you're getting any idea that there was something queer about Dad's death, you can discard it right now. Dad himself told Thibault to have the pool drained; it was a few days earlier than he usually had it cleaned, but the water was getting scummy. I know that's so, because I heard him give Thibault the order."

Campbell thought, I wonder who else might have overheard, or have known that the order was given? He said, "And you think he could have forgotten that the pool was being cleaned, and deliberately went out there and dived into seven inches of water?"

Naomi said, "He supposed the pool was filled again. It should have been."

"Who superintended the cleaning of the pool?"

"Ransome, the head gardener. As a matter of fact, it had been refilled, but it was a little higher than Dad liked it and that fool Ransome opened the gate again to lower the water, then went off and forgot to close it."

Campbell said, "Somebody closed it again, when the water was down to a few inches in depth."

"Certainly. Thibault closed it when he discovered that the pool was practically empty, even before he went on down toward the springboard calling for Dad. Ransome was lower than the ground when he learned what he'd done, but Thibault discharged him on the spot for criminal carelessness, without wages and without recommendation."

Campbell thought, This could all be true, and on the other hand it could be something else. Were she and Thibault in collusion, shielding somebody else and making Ransome the goat? It would be a pretty stupid man who could go out of the enclosure, lock the gate in the grille fence, and forget that he had left the sluice open. If Ransome were that dull-witted, would he have remained in Wark Andross' employ as head gardener for thirty years?

Campbell said, "You can really accept Wark's diving without noticing the water level?"

"There's an early moon now. I went out there to the pool myself and looked, after Thibault called me to tell me what had happened. The moon was low enough toward the west to shade that whole end of the pool, because of the windbreak.

Out toward the center where you could see the glimmer of the water, it was impossible to tell that it was any lower than it should be."

"Then it did strike you as a little strange that Wark wouldn't notice the lowered water?"

"Yes, it did—until I saw for myself. Look here, Pat!" Naomi sat erect and her eyes flashed indignation. "I know murder is your business, but that doesn't give you license to read murder into the most ordinary and unsuspicious circumstances. Dad would hate that."

Campbell said mildly, "I don't remember that I mentioned murder, Naomi."

The girl laughed shortly, and leaned back against the chaise. "What else could you possibly be hinting at?"

Campbell thought, I'd better go slow. I don't want to incur her antagonism—at least, not yet. He said, with some deprecation, "I suppose I'm merely so upset I don't realize how I sound. I know how Wark hated fuss, but it seemed a little on the rugged side to me—shushing up the hospital, possibly even delaying the report of his death to keep it out of the papers until after the cremation."

Naomi said, with a show of repressing pardonable impatience, "He didn't go to the hospital. That was just a little yarn to give the press something to talk about. Dad was dead when Thibault took him out of the pool. That was night before last. We called Dr. Wheeler immediately. He said Dad hadn't lived ten minutes after he struck the concrete head on. Dr. Wheeler reported the accidental death the next day, yesterday. We had Dad's body cremated yesterday, as he requested it should be done, the day after his death. Thibault telephoned the notice to the *Times*. If you want to know why he added a little touch of color regarding the hospital, ask him. I haven't considered it of enough importance to ask him myself."

Campbell said, "Don't get a mad on, Naomi. I didn't mean to irritate you. Perhaps you're right. I'm so used to dealing with murder where sudden death is concerned, perhaps I'm inclined to get out of step. I'd like to talk to Thibault, though, if you don't mind."

Relief was clear in the girl's lightened expression, in the warmer tone of her voice. "By all means talk to Thibault. I really wish you would. He can assure you that everything is as it seems to be, that nobody's hiding anything."

Campbell thought, Now why did she say that? I didn't accuse anyone of hiding anything. But he made no comment concerning the remark. He repeated his regret and shock at the loss of Wark Andross, took his leave of Naomi, and went out of the room in search of both Grannat and Thibault.

4

He heard from Grannat substantially the same things he had heard from Naomi. He had no doubt that Grannat was telling the truth, as far as he knew it; the trouble was, he didn't think Grannat knew all the truth. Whoever had wanted Wark out of the way would scarcely dare allow Grannat to learn anything that could be colored by the slightest suspicion; the old butler would never shield anyone who had brought harm to Wark Andross.

Campbell went on out to the patio enclosed by the two rear wings of the big house at the butler's invitation, and sat down in the shade with a cool drink Grannat brought him. Then the butler went in search of Thibault, and sent him out to the patio to talk to the big detective.

Thibault, too, told the same story, until it came to the matter of the hospital. Then he said matter-of-factly, "Miss Andross has the wrong impression, Mr. Campbell. You understand, I did not deliberately lie. When I heard Grannat calling Dr. Wheeler, I waited to hear what the doctor had said. Grannat told me Wheeler would be right out, and would hurry Mr. Andross to the hospital in case there was anything to be done. I had my hands full cleaning up and putting things to rights, and when I came upstairs Mr. Andross was gone. I took it for granted they had taken him to the hospital. I didn't know my error till the next day, until after I'd phoned the paper, and

Miss Andross told me it was a good enough story for the papers, but the body had been taken right to the undertaker's."

Campbell thought the story had the glibness of words ready on the tongue, but he made no remark to that effect. He said, "Didn't you realize that Mr. Andross was dead when you found him?"

"Why, no. No, sir, I didn't." Thibault was a thin, gray man, and his face was habitually bleak, but he seemed to be talking easily and without reservation, perhaps a little too easily. "He was still warm. I couldn't feel any pulse, and I knew he was badly injured, but I thought he might still be alive. I've heard of accident victims still being alive after even the doctor thought them quite dead."

Campbell thought, At last something tangible, something to tie on to. Andross had not been cold when Thibault found him. "How long had he been out at the pool when you grew uneasy and went to look for him, Thibault?"

"Well over an hour and a half, Mr. Campbell. That was what set me wondering. He was invariably through with his swim, back in the house and ready for his drink within three quarters of an hour."

"And was he in the habit of sitting around in his bathing trunks till the last minute, diving in and swimming once the length of the pool, then coming immediately into the house?"

"Why, no, sir! He went right in, and spent all of the time in the water. He—" Thibault stared sharply for an instant, then he said, "Oh!"

Campbell said, "That's right. If he'd dived when he first went out—and the doctor says he didn't live ten minutes after he crashed into the concrete—even in seven inches of water he'd have been stone cold when you found him. What was he doing all that time he was supposed to be swimming?"

"I don't know, Mr. Campbell. Talking to somebody, I suppose. You—" Thibault stopped short, then he said hoarsely, "You think he was murdered, don't you?"

"I'm getting surer of it every minute. Any likely suspects to suggest?"

Thibault said, "Everybody who had access to the grille-gate key, and that means everybody on the place. Everybody knew where it was kept."

"Yes? And where was it kept?"

"In that little iron box on the steel post the gate locks onto; too high for any child to reach, but handy for any adult who wanted to take a swim in deep water."

"Do you know of any person who had any motive to get rid of Mr. Andross?"

Thibault's voice suddenly sounded strained. "You suspect me, don't you?"

Campbell said, "I suspect everybody. I have to."

"You're sure in your own mind he was murdered?"

"I was sure as soon as I'd talked to Mr. Freedon and knew how Andross met his death."

The two men were sitting on a bench, turned so that they faced each other. Thibault's gray face had turned slowly pasty. Anger and wild grief showed for an instant in his eyes, in his voice. He said violently, "If I could get hold of the son of a bitch who did it, I'd strangle him with my own hands." There was no doubting his sincerity, and in that moment Campbell knew he had found one man who would tell him the truth, who had told him the truth, and who would prove a dependable ally.

The detective said quietly, "So would I, if I followed my own inclinations. Let's take it a little cooler, and strangle him with the hangman's noose—metaphorically speaking, since we have the gas chamber in California. Get hold of yourself, Thibault. You can be a great deal of help to me if you'll keep your head."

Thibault said, "Yes, sir. Anything I can do. I probably knew Mr. Andross better than anybody else, even his own daughter. He used to confide in me a lot. He relied on me. I wouldn't protect anybody who had harmed him, any more than Grannat would. You can count on both of us. I wouldn't swear that you can count on anybody else in the house."

Campbell asked, "Even Miss Naomi Andross?"

Thibault said tonelessly, "I said anybody in the house."

"Okay, Thibault. Anybody in the house it is. But I'll need to know just how much territory that takes in. Andross usually had a lot of people around him. The house seems pretty deserted today. I haven't seen anybody but you and Grannat and Miss Andross."

"Yes, sir. It is deserted. Everybody's gone, even the maids and the footmen; they went out to the Canyon House to get it brightened up and ready for the will reading. The servants went to do the work; the guests went because they didn't like to stay here after Mr. Andross' death. Miss Andross suggested that they go, she wanted to be alone for a few days. She and I will drive out with Mr. Freedon next Tuesday."

"I see. And who were the guests this time? How many of them are there?"

"There are seven of them, Mr. Campbell. Jewell Northrup and Ike Northrup, Miss Naomi's uncle and aunt on her mother's side. They only came down from Seattle for a visit, but I've an idea they'll stay now. You've met Martin Quest, Mr. Andross' cousin, haven't you? Wasn't he living here already the last time you came to see Mr. Andross?"

"Yes. He was. I remember Quest."

"Then there's Ranny Overholt—he's a friend of Mr. Quest, come to stay the summer; Francie Dunham, who's engaged to Mr. Quest; Sally Mace who's a friend of Miss Dunham and Miss Andross; and Mr. Quentin Ireland, who's been pursuing Miss Andross and would like to take her away from Mr. Freedon. That's the lot of them."

"Just how intimately would any of them be concerned with Mr. Andross? Any of them have any motive to want him dead that you know of?"

"I couldn't rightly say, Mr. Campbell, if I'm going to stick to the truth and what I know. I suppose Mr. and Mrs. Northrup and Mr. Quest all expect to be remembered in the will. Mrs. Northrup was sister to Mrs. Andross, and I'd judge they were pretty fond of each other. Mr. Andross and Mr. Quest got along, but I suppose you'd know that."

Campbell said, "Yes, I know. Wark thought a good deal of Martin. I liked Martin myself. I still do, if he hasn't changed. And the others?"

"Well, that's all I know about them, Mr. Campbell. Simply guests, friends. If any of them could have a reason to want Mr. Andross out of the way, I don't know it."

"Where were they all when Mr. Andross was killed?"

"Oh, scattered here and there about the grounds. Not even Miss Naomi was in the house."

"I see. Well, if that's all you can think of to tell me right now, Thibault, we'll have to let it rest there till we meet at the Canyon House."

"You'll be there, Mr. Campbell?"

"I will; at Wark Andross' special request. Do you know anything about the terms of the will, Thibault?"

"No, sir, I don't. I suppose Mr. Freedon is the only one who knows just what's in it."

"Any other heirs you can think of?"

"No. Mr. Quest and Miss Naomi were Mr. Andross' only living relatives so far as I know. And Mr. and Mrs. Northrup are the only other relatives from Miss Naomi's mother's side."

"I guess that about ties it up then, Thibault." Campbell rose from the patio bench, leaving beside Thibault the empty glass he had been holding idly. The little pieces of ice tinkled in the glass as he set it down. "If you hear or uncover anything I ought to know, give me a ring. And keep strictly to yourself everything touched on in this little discussion we've just ended. Don't let anybody find out that I'm on the trail of Mr. Andross' murderer."

"No, sir; I'll not say a word. You can depend on me. But— maybe I had better tell you this. Have you ever been out to the Canyon House, Mr. Campbell?"

"No, I haven't. Why?"

"Mr. Andross was very fond of the Canyon House. He said it was the kind of place where he'd like to live. I think he always hoped to go there to spend the last of his days. Miss Naomi doesn't like it. She hates the country. She says it's too quiet and lonely; she much prefers the town house. She swears she'll sell the Canyon House, or set fire to it if she isn't allowed to sell it. Mr. Andross didn't want it sold. He said he had a special use for it, but I don't know what it was unless he meant to go and live there. I always thought that was what he meant by a special use for the Canyon House."

"No, it wasn't, Thibault. I know what he meant. Don't worry. The Canyon House will not be sold, and it will not be burned down. It will fulfill the destiny Mr. Andross intended for it."

"I'm very happy to hear that, Mr. Campbell." Thibault also

had risen from the bench, and he fell into step beside Campbell as the detective turned to leave the patio and go back to
his car. "I'd been troubled about it. I'm not likely to see you
again until next Tuesday, I suppose?"

"Not likely, Thibault, unless something turns up. By the
way, where were Mr. Andross' ashes scattered, do you know?"

"Yes, sir. I scattered them. Under the cypress trees, around
the pool. None of the others knows. They'd rather not know.
You wouldn't like to see the pool and the board?"

"No. He didn't dive from the springboard, Thibault. He
was slugged and thrown in. I have good reason for being sure
of that. There are several little things we may go into later if
it seems advisable, but that's all for the present. See you Tuesday, then, Thibault. Oh, by the way—did you close the sluice
when you found Mr. Andross?"

"No, sir!" Thibault answered emphatically. "I did not!"

Campbell left the patio behind, rounded the end of the
northern wing of the house, and walked past the shallow pool
toward the dark bulk of the cypress windbreak. He had no in-
tention of leaving the hill until after he had carefully looked
over the spot where Wark Andross had met his death. But he
didn't want Thibault or anyone else along, and had he told
Thibault he was going to see the pool he might have had an
awkward minute preventing the man from accompanying him.
Besides, he didn't want anyone to know he was examining the
enclosure, even Thibault. He was glad the key was kept so
handy.

Within a few minutes he was beyond sight inside the rec-
tangle screened by the windbreak. He got the key out of the
iron box on the steel gatepost, unlocked the gate and went
into the pool area. As the gate swung shut, he discovered that

it was self-locking. He went on toward the end of the pool, dropping the key into his pocket.

The pool had been filled again. Now it lay placid in the sun, like a sheet of molten glass. Campbell stopped by the springboard from which Andross was supposed to have dived and stood looking down into the water. Nothing was there to tell him anything of what had taken place. Whatever instrument had been used to crush Wark Andross' skull had been taken away; there was no story written in blood or prints on the smooth face of the tile. Campbell asked himself what he had expected to find: anyone clever enough to take advantage of the perfect situation for murder would not leave traces.

The detective went on to the other end of the pool. Here, to one side, was a roomy bath house, with racks for towels and wet bathing suits. Near the farther wall of the bath house was a small rectangular well in the tile flooring, and thrust up from the well was the mechanism for draining the pool. The intake was at the other end of the bath house. Campbell inspected both mechanisms closely; they were almost identical, still no one could have mistaken one for the other. One was labeled plainly in large orange letters against the dark green paint, INTAKE. The other was labeled in bright green letters against dark red paint, OUTLET.

Both the water gate of the intake and the sluice gate of the outlet were operated by stout iron levers, similar to an old-fashioned pump handle. The detective experimented with the sluice gate lever. The mechanism was simple; a steel gate on the end of a steel pole. One pushed down on the iron handle, and the sluice gate rose to let the water pour out. One dragged up on the handle, the long pole shoved down and the sluice closed. It did not work easily, and Campbell judged that was for a purpose: no child could have operated it, few women could. It needed a stout arm to lift or lower the sluice gate.

Campbell walked slowly out of the bath house. He had learned what he wanted to know. No one could possibly have shoved that handle down and left the sluice open by accident. No one had done it by accident. The detective told himself that Ransome hadn't gone off and forgotten that he'd left the sluice open, either; he'd bet on it. In several respects, Naomi's story was too thin. It—Campbell smiled wryly at the play on words—it didn't hold water.

He walked on down the tiled pathway along the pool, turning the whole matter over in his mind. He thought he could guess pretty closely what had happened. Someone had heard Wark order the pool drained and cleaned, or had learned of the order through a third person. The killer had known of Wark's moonlight swims, he had seen the fortuitous opportunity as a Godsend, no doubt. But the pool had been filled again too soon, so the murderer had promptly slipped into the enclosure and reopened the sluice on the sly. When the pool was lowered enough to suit his purpose, he had closed the sluice, and waited for Wark to go out for his nightly swim.

But what had Wark been doing all that hour and over, between the time he went to the pool and the time Thibault had discovered his body? It might be of particular importance to know that, Campbell thought. Maybe the murderer hadn't found it too easy to maneuver Wark Andross into a position where he could be struck squarely on top of the head. Wark hadn't been a tall man, but such a blow could be an awkward thing to achieve.

Campbell stopped at the grille gate, unlocked it and went out of the enclosure, returned the key to the iron box and went on to his car. He wondered whether Eilers had been successful with his leg work.

5

He found Eilers in the office waiting for him. Eilers started to speak, but Campbell said, "Just a minute, Rick. I want to talk to Dr. Wheeler, then we'll get down to business." He sat down at Eilers' desk and called the doctor's number. Eilers waited, listening to Campbell's half of the conversation.

When he had Wheeler on the telephone, Campbell told the doctor how he had known nothing of Wark's death till he had seen it in the newspaper, and how he had called Freedon. "Freedon told me about your rushing Wark to the hospital—"

"He didn't get that from me," Wheeler interrupted. "I don't know how that story got into the paper. It's not true. Andross was dead when I reached the house. He was dead when Thibault took him out of the pool. He never knew a thing after his head hit the concrete. I took Andross' body to the undertaker's in the back of my sedan, at Naomi Andross' urgent request. She didn't want an ambulance screaming up the hill and attracting attention. She's as bad about hating fuss as her father was. I don't know where Thibault got that idea about the hospital."

Campbell said, "Oh, simply enough. You did tell Grannat you'd rush Wark to the hospital if anything was to be done, didn't you?"

"I did. But there was nothing to be done."

"No, of course not. Thibault didn't know that. He was busy, and when he came in and found the body gone, he simply took it for granted you'd taken Wark to a hospital. What time were you called to the Andross house?"

"It was ten-fifteen when I left home. I reached Andross' place at ten-forty-five."

"About how long had Wark been dead then?"

"Oh, an hour, possibly. Not more than an hour, perhaps less. Why? See here, Campbell, you aren't trying to make anything more of this than the simple accident it was, are you? Remember, more people—"

"I know," Campbell cut in dryly, "more people are killed in home accidents than in any other kind. Wark Andross was my friend. I was interested in knowing the particulars of his death, that's all."

"Oh, I see." Wheeler's voice sounded mollified. "Well, that's all there is to it. Andross ordered the pool drained and cleaned, forgot he'd given the order, didn't notice the lowered level in the dark, and dived into seven inches of water. All subsequent details were taken care of with the dispatch and total lack of publicity he himself had requested. Anything more I can tell you?"

Campbell said, "I think not. Thanks very much," and put down the telephone.

Eilers said, "Learn anything?"

"I learned plenty, for a starter, at least. But, first, how'd you come out?"

"No trouble at all. Everything checked. Elizabeth Anne Holloway died two years ago of double pneumonia. No Elizabeth Holloway was born in San Francisco on September the fifteenth, 1918; no Holloway at all was born in San Francisco September the fifteenth, 1918, or on the fourteenth or sixteenth either. A marriage license was issued in L.A. on February the tenth, 1926, to E. A. Holloway, legal, and E. R. Holloway, legal. That's why you didn't find anything when you were looking for a license issued to Elizabeth Anne Andross. She took her maiden name back, long enough to secure a marriage license, anyhow."

"You check any further?"

"Yeah. Both Holloways were listed as living in L.A. I looked in the city directory. I didn't find any E. A. Holloway, or any Andross. I did find Ethan Roy Holloway. Subsequent to the issuing of the marriage license, he'd changed his address. I went out and looked up the change of address. It had been twenty years since he'd lived there, and I didn't have much hope of finding anything, but I ran into one of those streaks of luck that pop up now and then for the private eye."

"Good! What did you find?"

"An ancient rooming house, and a little old landlady almost as ancient as her house. She's been running the place for thirty years. She was a little wary of me at first, but when I told her I was just trying to track down an old friend, she opened up and got real chummy. Remembered Elizabeth Anne, perfectly; had reason to remember her. It seems that in those days Elizabeth Anne did pen sketches, and she'd given a couple to the landlady, suitably framed. The old lady showed me the sketches. They were damned good too; looked like wood-cuts."

"The sketches were her reason for remembering Elizabeth Anne?"

"Yep. The old lady said the lodger had come there under the name of Elizabeth Anne Andross, and with a little girl about seven years old, named Mary. But right away she'd had the little girl drop the Mary. She told the old lady she wanted to call her by her second name; the kid had been named for her. But two Elizabeths might have proved slightly confusing, so she called the little girl Bess from then on. While she was still rooming there, Mrs. Andross had married Ethan Roy Holloway, and they had continued to live there until Holloway died, around two or three years later. Then Mrs. Holloway and Bess moved away and the landlady never heard of them again. She'd always sort of wondered what had become of them. She was sorry she couldn't tell me any more."

Campbell said, "Good work, kid. That ties that up. Bess is Wark's daughter, Mary. There's no possible doubt left."

Eilers listened in interested silence as Campbell went on to relate what he had learned at the Andross house, and to repeat his recent telephone conversation with Dr. Wheeler. Then the detective said, "I don't want it to get around, as I said before, that suspicion has been raised in any quarter. It won't get around. Naomi isn't going to tell anyone, unless she takes the trouble to warn the murderer. If she's shielding him, she may grow uneasy enough to let something drop without realizing what she's doing. Thibault won't talk, but he'll be on the alert; I don't imagine anything significant will get by him."

"Looks like Naomi's getting herself all wound up, doesn't it?"

Campbell said grimly, "She's lying faster than a horse can trot; I'm morally certain of it, but I want to prove it before we go out to the Canyon House Tuesday. She's already done a little fancy yarn-twisting. She tells Doc Wheeler that Wark forgot he'd ordered the pool drained. She tells me Wark expected the pool to be refilled, that it had been refilled and then Ransome went off and forgot he left the sluice open."

Eilers said, "You know, she might have gotten away with it, easily, if you hadn't stuck your suspicious nose in."

"Sure. Of course she'd have gotten away with it. It looks like a perfectly straightforward story to Doc Wheeler. He isn't going around running off at the head about what he has readily accepted as a common home accident. She probably told the same yarn to the house guests. They wouldn't give it another thought. The same applies to Grannat, the footman and the maids. Suspicion hadn't occurred to Thibault, until I jogged him into thinking. Sure she'd have gotten away with it. But not now, brother! The whole set-up stinks, from where I now sit. On two counts I'm going to prove Naomi a liar before Tuesday."

"Two?"

"Right. Ransome and the moon. Three, in fact. Thibault *didn't* close the sluice though Naomi told me he did."

"How you going to get hold of Ransome?"

"I'm not. You are. I have other fish to fry. Call up all the employment agencies, tell 'em you want to hire a gardener, you want an experienced gardener with good references. Tell 'em you'd particularly like to get hold of one man you know to be expert in his line. Give 'em Ransome's name, Gerald Ransome. If they don't have Ransome listed, tell 'em you'll call back. I'll be in my office. Let me know what you find out."

Campbell rose from behind Eilers' desk, and as he went through the inter-office door to his own quarters he heard Eilers beginning his telephone work. The detective sat down behind his own desk and opened the red ledger. He took his desk pen from its holder and began setting down the data he had collected concerning Bess Andross and the death of her father. He was still engaged in the same task when Eilers came in to report.

"Ransome isn't listed with any of the agencies now, Pat."

Campbell looked up, holding his pen poised above the red ledger. "Then put an ad in the *Times'* want ad column, to run the rest of the week. Gardener, with experience in the best homes, position of responsibility, permanent job at top wages, live on the premises. Have applicants call at this office. Stall everybody else; when Ransome comes in, send him to me."

"You think it'll draw him?"

"I'm sure of it. He'll scarcely have another job this quick. If it doesn't, we'll try something else."

"But, if he was discharged for criminal carelessness, just to provide Naomi with a goat—"

"Don't worry; he wasn't. Thibault didn't discharge him. If he had he would have mentioned it when he was talking to me. There's another place Miss Naomi lied. I doubt that Thibault knows anything about Ransome being discharged as yet. I didn't mention it when I was talking to him. He's a kind of simple little guy, I didn't want his mind covering too much territory. I figured I could take care of Ransome. Setting Thibault to worrying about how the pool happened to be emptied the second time wouldn't accomplish anything. Get that ad in, in time for tomorrow morning's paper. Tomorrow's Thursday. We have to work fast."

Eilers went back to his own office to telephone in the wanted advertisement. Campbell continued writing in the red ledger. Nothing more of any significance transpired before the two men left the office to eat dinner and go home for the night.

The detective reached his apartment to find Drake Freedon waiting for him. Freedon said, "I want to talk to you in private, Campbell, so I came here where no one would be around to overhear, even Eilers."

Campbell said, "That's fine. Come on in. Have a drink with me?"

Freedon sighed. "I could stand a cool one. We had a long spring this year, but it's surely warming up now."

They went into Campbell's living room, and Freedon lounged in a deep armchair while Campbell prepared the drinks. Freedon was a tall young man, a couple of inches over six feet, with wide shoulders and a compact muscular build. His hair was thick and straight and glossy. He was of black Scotch ancestry, and his pale blue eyes and very white teeth contrasted noticeably with his dark skin, jet-black hair and brows. He took the cocktail Campbell brought, smiled and swallowed a mouthful with relish.

Campbell dropped into a chair opposite the lawyer, lighted a cigarette and offered Freedon one. "What's on your mind, Drake?"

Freedon answered without preamble. "I don't think it was an accident, Campbell. I think Wark Andross was murdered. I thought a lot of Wark, and he liked me. I want you to get the man who killed him. I'll pay your fee out of my own pocket."

Campbell said, "You can forget about the fee. Wark was a friend of mine, too. What makes you think he was murdered?"

Freedon smiled sardonically. "Because so many people wanted him dead, five that I know of, and he wanted to live. And all five of them were in the house when he was killed. I mean they were living in the house and would have been around the grounds somewhere. Any one of them could have raised the sluice gate and emptied the pool. Have you talked to Naomi yet?"

"Yes, I was out there this afternoon."

"She tell you Ransome forgot he left the sluice open and Thibault shut it when he went in to look for Andross?"

"Yes. That's exactly what she told me."

"You don't believe that, do you?"

Campbell shook his head. "No. Ransome wasn't that careless. And I can't see Thibault stopping to notice the water level and hurrying to shut the sluice gate when he was worried about Andross and trying to find him. I can't see him giving a second thought to shutting the sluice even after he discovered the water level and found Wark's body. As a story it's ridiculous, and if Naomi herself believes it she's being a trifle absurd."

Freedon said with a little flare of anger, "She expects me to believe anything she tells me, and I have to pretend to believe if I expect to keep peace in the family. We haven't been getting along well for some time, but Wark didn't know it. He wanted me in the family, and I might even have gone on and married her if he'd lived. Now, wild horses couldn't drag me to the altar with Naomi Andross."

"Who are the five people you spoke of, and why should they want Wark dead?"

Freedon said, "They're named in his will, that's why. They want the money, and want it bad, all of them. You know how much money Wark left, Campbell?"

"Not exactly. Is it pertinent?"

"Very. He left eight million dollars in cash and negotiable securities. He told me you knew the terms of the will, but do you know all of them?"

"No. Not concerning the smaller bequests."

"But you did know he had another daughter? You did know he had divided the bulk of his estate between Naomi and the other girl, Mary, if Mary could be found. He told me he'd had you trying to trace her for years. You ever track her down?"

Campbell smiled somberly. "Yes. I'll have her out there at the Canyon House, Tuesday, to hear the will read." He explained how Bess Andross had come to the office that morning with the clippings her mother had saved. "Ironical, isn't it? He wanted to see her so badly, and only his death could bring her to him."

Freedon said, "God, I'm glad you got hold of her at last. She sounds pretty regular. I'm glad for his sake. Maybe he knows. I like to think it's possible. Well, to answer your questions; we'll come back to Bess later. Wark liked simple, round figures. Three million in cash and securities, along with the Beverly Hills place, to Naomi. The same in cash and securities, along with the Canyon House, to Bess. That leaves two million to spread around among five relatives and eighteen servants. You might as well know all about the will right now, it will give you something to figure on. How do you want it?"

"Let's have the servants first."

"Very well." Freedon paused to take another swallow of his drink. "Four maids, two footmen and four gardeners at the Beverly Hills place; three gardeners, caretaker and housekeeper —man and wife—at the Canyon House: all fifteen of them receive ten thousand each—Wark was no piker—and the privilege of remaining in Andross employ as long as they desire. Grannat, Thibault and Ransome, all with Wark for years, affectionately regarded and fully trusted, each receives twenty thousand, and is never to be discharged for any cause whatsoever. That brings us up to two hundred and ten thousand."

Campbell thought, So he doesn't yet know that Ransome

has already been discharged. He said nothing about it; that could be discussed later.

Freedon went on. "Now as to the five relatives. To the two Northrups, Naomi's maternal aunt and uncle, Wark left five hundred thousand. I was talking to Naomi this morning. She said they'd all gone to the Canyon House till after the will is read, but they were at Beverly Hills when Wark was killed. You know Mart Quest, I think?"

"Wark's cousin? Yes. He seems like a nice fellow."

Freedon said with enthusiasm, "He's a great lad. Wark loved him like a brother. Wark left Quest a million even. Mart Quest's mother was sister to Wark Andross' father. When old Quest died, Mrs. Quest married Overholt."

"Ranny's father?"

"Yes. Ranny was then two years old; a former marriage of Overholt's. Therefore, Ranny is no relation at all to Martin Quest, but they grew up together and Mart always considered Ranny his brother. Francie Dunham, who is Mart's fiancée, is a distant cousin of the same family branch. Neither Ranny nor Francie was really related to Wark Andross, but he thought so much of Mart that he counted them in with the family. Therefore I class them with the relatives. Wark bequeathed each of them a hundred thousand. That leaves ninety thousand out of the two million he was, he said, going to spread around among people who had it coming, because they were real people, or simply because he liked them. Any idea whom he left that ninety thousand to?"

Campbell's eyes twinkled. "I expect he left it to one Drake Freedon."

Freedon said, smiling, "Yes, most of it, in spite of my protestations that I didn't need it, had plenty of my own. He left you five thousand, for services rendered. He also left you that collection of guns you always admired so much."

Campbell said soberly, amazed, "I never dreamed he intended doing a thing like that. I was already well paid. I shall treasure the guns."

"Yes. He knew you would." Freedon's smile lingered.

"And that rounds it out?"

"Yes—there it is; any of those legacies, even the smallest, means a lot of money to those who inherit it, is ample incentive for murder. But, none of the servants had the least idea what he might receive, if anything. Not one of them would have laid a hand on Wark Andross, anyhow. He took care of them, they had everything they wanted and a happy existence. They're all out of it. Your suspects have to be the five relatives, and the only one of those I'd like to exclude is Martin Quest. But I can't exclude Mart. He lived with Wark at Wark's request, but he isn't a money maker. If Wark had left him nothing and Naomi kicked him out, he'd be stony broke; like Francie and Ranny and the Northrups, poor as Job's turkey and nothing to look forward to."

Campbell said, "He could work."

Freedon laughed shortly. "He could, but he won't. He hates work. He asks nothing better of life than to live, and live well, hunt and fish and sleep in the sun. Don't mistake me; I like Mart, but he's lazy as hell and we have to take everything into consideration."

"How about Francie's parents, and Ranny's?" Campbell questioned.

"Francie's parents are divorced, married again, fight like cats and dogs and skate on the thin edge, always in debt. Ranny's parents are both dead. He's a lot like Mart, likable and nice `o have around, but he'll never get anywhere on his own steam. Now you won't have to keep your ear cocked to hear the will read at the Canyon House. You can give your attention to the legatees and to catching the killer we have with us. There you have it; what do you think?"

Campbell said slowly, "I don't indulge in snap judgments. I'm very glad to get all this information, but I'll have to sleep on it before I know what I think. I suppose you got it from Wark?"

"Yes. Everything I know about the family, I know from him."

"What do you know about Elizabeth Anne Holloway and Bess?"

"Not a damn thing. You were the only one he talked to about them. All he ever told me was that he had a daughter Mary by a former marriage and you were hired to find her. The only reason he ever told me that much was so I'd understand the will. I never knew anything further till you told me a little while ago about Bess."

Campbell said, "I'd better tell you something else. Ransome has already been fired, for criminal carelessness in leaving a drained pool for Wark to dive into. So Naomi says. She says Thibault fired him. I don't believe it. Thibault wouldn't exceed his authority that way in the first place."

Freedon laughed. "You're damned right he wouldn't. And if he'd tried it, Ransome would have told him to go to hell. The same goes for Grannat. She fired him herself, and you can bet on it. Nobody ever had any right to fire Grannat, Ransome or Thibault but Wark Andross; nobody but Naomi would have the authority since Wark is gone. But she can't do that. Something's pretty rotten somewhere; Ransome's the last man on earth to be guilty of criminal carelessness. We've got to get him back. We've—"

Campbell interrupted. "You can leave Ransome to me. I'll get him."

"Well, I guess that's all I have to say. Only, are you going to play along with me? Have I convinced you that Wark was murdered?"

Campbell said quietly, "I've known it ever since I called you this morning and you told me how he died. I haven't let the subject rest for a minute since. I won't let it rest until I get my man, or woman, or both."

Freedon surveyed the detective narrowly as he got to his feet. "Both, eh? Maybe you've got something there. It probably would take two to get around him without raising his suspicions and spoiling their neat little plan. Wark was no man's fool. What do you think about that drained pool business anyhow?"

Campbell rose, to walk with the lawyer to the door. "I don't think they ever intended that he should dive into seven inches of water, Drake. They only wanted it to look as if he had, stage setting for the act."

"That's what I think, too. Thanks a lot for listening to me talk your arm off. I'll see you at the Canyon House, Tuesday, then."

Campbell said, "Right. Anything else comes up you think I should know in the meantime, give me a buzz."

"I'll do that. Good night, Pat."

"Good night, Drake." Campbell closed the door after the departing lawyer and turned back into the room. He still felt a little dazed at Andross' bequest to him, and infinitely touched.

He walked slowly over to a chair, sat down, stretched his legs out before him and closed his eyes. He needed to do a lot of thinking. It was past midnight before he roused himself and went to bed, as tired as if he'd done a day's hard manual labor. He went to sleep a trifle angry with himself for being no nearer to a solution of the problem than when he had said good night to Drake Freedon.

6

THE NEXT DAY, THURSDAY the eleventh, brought no word from Gerald Ransome, and nothing new developed to shed more light on the case.

As soon as darkness fell that evening, Campbell backed his car out of the apartment house garage and drove downtown. He killed the early evening at a picture show, had a light supper at the Brown Derby, and at a little after eleven o'clock he drove up into the Hollywood hills. On the crest of one thinly populated hill, he got out of the blue coupe and paced the open ground to the east of a stand of trees. He had chosen the spot with care. The trees were about twenty feet high.

Patrick Campbell was watching the moon. It was round and full and big. He remembered making some remark to Eilers about Wark seeing the lowered water level after dark with none too bright a moon. He wondered how he had got the idea that Luna wasn't up to standard at this time of the month. The orb was bright enough, but it was low to the south. The sky was a dim, pale blue, only a few scattered stars were visible. He glanced at the luminous dial of his watch. Eleven fifty-three.

He stayed there on the hill, pacing by the stand of trees, enjoying the cool fresh air, until one o'clock. He could still see the moon at the tops of the trees to the west, trees the same approximate height as the cypress windbreak around the pool. He laughed softly to himself, and went back to his car.

He said aloud, in an amused undertone, "So, the moon was low enough to the west to shade the whole end of the pool where the springboard was because of the windbreak, was it? Lie Number One proved and nailed down, Miss Naomi Andross. It would have taken Doc Wheeler a few minutes to get ready after he was called, and he had left home at ten-fifteen. It would have taken Thibault a good half hour to get Andross out of the pool and into the house before he called Wheeler. Doc said Wark had been dead about an hour when he reached the Andross house at ten-forty-five. Therefore Wark was killed at about a quarter to ten, had been dead only a few minutes when Thibault found him."

Campbell thumbed the starter, put the car in motion and started down the hill, still talking to himself. "And Naomi went out then to check on the moon. It would have been shining right down into the pool! I hope to hell Ransome will show up tomorrow, and give me a chance to nail lie Number Two. From what Freedon says, it looks like a cinch already; but it isn't proved so. Maybe there's a dim possibility that Thibault did exceed his authority, and fire Ransome and Ransome took it, and Thibault didn't think to mention it when he was talking to me, but it sounds pretty wild. We'll see what Ransome says."

The next day three men came in in the morning to see about the gardener job. Eilers asked their names, then said regretfully, "Sorry, the position's already filled. But we'll keep you in mind if this man doesn't suit and we have another opening."

Early in the afternoon another man came to inquire, a man

whom Eilers thought he had seen out at Andross' Beverly Hills home; a medium-height man with thick shoulders and stout arms, a little stooped, his skin deeply browned by exposure to the weather. There were fine wrinkles about his gray eyes and a white patch across his forehead next to the roots of his gray hair where a strip had been shaded from the sun.

He walked up to Eilers' desk with the confidence of a man who knows his worth in his chosen profession. "You advertised for an experienced gardener?"

Eilers said, "We did. Are you Gerald Ransome?"

The gardener looked a bit surprised. "Why, yes. I am. Why?"

Eilers nodded toward the inter-office door. "In there, please. Mr. Campbell would like to see you."

Ransome hesitated, the expression of his face having grown somewhat troubled. "He was a friend of Mr. Wark Andross, wasn't he?"

Eilers said, "That's right. You needn't be apprehensive. He only wants to ask you a few questions."

Ransome said with a slightly wry smile, "That's what I was afraid of." He went on into Campbell's office.

Campbell looked up with smiling cordiality. "Good afternoon, Ransome. Glad you came. I was beginning to be afraid you were deliberately staying away."

"I did, for a while, then I thought I'd better come." Ransome seated himself in the clients' chair, balancing his hat on his knee. "After I read in the paper about Mr. Andross' death, and then saw your ad, it struck me there might be something queer about it. But you draw a blank in me. I don't know anything. I wasn't there. I'd been fired."

Campbell said quickly, "You don't mean you'd been fired before Mr. Andross was killed!"

"Well, I'm not sure, but I guess maybe I was. You see, I didn't live on the place; all the quarters were taken up by the other servants. Mr. Andross said he'd put up a little house for me and my wife, but I told him never mind. We live up in the hills, couple of miles or so beyond the Andross place. So all I had to do was take my hat and walk out when I was fired."

"And when were you fired, Ransome?"

"Monday evening, same day Andross died. But the papers didn't say much, only that he died in the hospital before midnight. I ain't sure I was canned before he died, because I don't know just when he died or what kind of accident took him off."

"What time in the evening were you discharged, Ransome? Who fired you? Thibault?"

"Why, no, Mr. Campbell! Thibault wouldn't have had any authority to give me my walkin' papers! It was Mr. Andross himself as fired me; that is, he gave the orders, though they was delivered by Miss Naomi, same as he'd tell Thibault to have me drain the pool or take down a tree that was getting in the way, or something. It was just about dark, and ordinarily I'd have been on my way home, but I'd stayed to hone the blades of the power-mower; it was a bit dull, and I intended cutting the lawn the next day. I always like to get up early and do the mowing while it's cool. Mr. Andross never would have mechanics around the place, you know; what we wanted repaired we did ourselves or sent out. He never even had a chauffeur on the place, said they were a damned nuisance and anyway he liked to do his own driving. So'd Miss Naomi."

"It would have been around seven, to seven-thirty or eight, then that she told you you'd have to go?"

"Around there somewhere, before eight, I'd say; it wasn't quite dark yet. I never thought nothing of it. Mr. Andross half the time sent his orders through her or Thibault, and sometimes Grannat. And that was about the time he usually liked to go out to the pool, anywhere from eight to nine, if there was a moon. He didn't care so much for night swimmin' if there was no moon."

"What excuse did Miss Andross make for firing you?"

"Oh, it wasn't nothing I'd done, Mr. Campbell," Ransome assured earnestly. "I always gave satisfaction. I'd been with him ever since he built the Beverly Hills place. Miss Andross said they were going to sell the place and live in the Canyon House, and they wouldn't be needing me any more. I didn't think nothing of that, either; I'd known how Mr. Andross always wanted to live in the Canyon House and she wouldn't. I was just glad she'd come to see it his way at last. I said so. I said I could get another job, and I hoped they'd all be happy in the Canyon House. And Miss Andross gave me my full month's wages, and six months' wages bonus, all in cash. Which didn't surprise me—that was Mr. Andross' way, he always paid well, and if he ever had to let a man go he gave him a bonus big enough to hold him up until he got another job."

"She told you the cash was from Mr. Andross?"

"Yes, sir. That's why I'm sure I must have been fired before he was killed. If anything had been wrong like that, she'd have told me. She had queer ways sometimes, and I got the idea once in a while that she didn't like me much. But she's honest, and I'm sure she'd have told me if she'd got word he'd been hurt in an accident."

"She gave you a reference?"

"Oh, yes! Dictated by Mr. Andross, and signed for Mr. Andross by herself. I couldn't ask for a better reference." He hesitated, then went on with some deference, "I can understand why there was no more in the papers. That was the way Mr. Andross would have wanted it. My Lord, how that man hated fuss and publicity about his personal affairs! But I'd like awful well to know just how he died, if you know, and would be kind enough to tell me."

"I'll tell you by asking a few questions, Ransome. Be sure that you answer me carefully and accurately."

"I'll do my best, Mr. Campbell."

"Did Mr. Andross, through Thibault, give you orders to drain and clean the pool earlier than you were in the habit of doing?"

"Well, I don't know as I'd state it just that way; we cleaned the pool whenever it needed cleaning. In the hot weather we always had to clean it oftener, of course; it would get scummy fast, and Mr. Andross hated to swim in water that had chlorine in it."

"You never put chlorine in the big pool, then?"

"No, sir. Never. I hadn't noticed it needed cleaning again so soon, that's a fact. So Mr. Andross sent me word by Thibault to take care of it, Saturday night just as I was leaving to go home. I said I'd attend to it right away the next day."

"That would be Sunday?"

"Yes, sir. I drove over Sunday morning about nine o'clock and opened the sluice gate. Then I went back home to spend the day with my wife, as I always do on Sunday."

"How long did it take the pool to drain, Ransome?"

"Well, you know how Mr. Andross always wanted everything to be convenient; when the pool was built he wanted the sluice and intake gates to be big enough so it wouldn't take forever to drain and fill the pool ready for swimming again. Both intake and outlet are damn big, but even at that it takes around nine to ten hours to drain it, and the same to fill it. Taking in the cleaning, it's about twenty-four hours' time after you open the sluice gate till it's ready to swim in again."

"I see. Go on, Ransome. Tell me the exact procedure at this particular time."

"Well, opening the sluice at nine Sunday morning, I knew the water'd all be drained out about six that evening. So I came back at six and started work on it. Mr. Andross never swam much on Sundays; always a lot of company around and he spent his time with them. It was a good time to drain the big pool. I worked till dark, but I didn't get it done. I left a few inches of water in the bottom and went home. But I knew Mr. Andross would sure want to go swimming on Monday night since there was a good moon, so I came back Monday morning about one o'clock and finished cleaning the pool by floodlight."

"And when did you start refilling it?"

"Right around two A.M., Mr. Campbell. I wanted to get it full before noon, so it could lay all afternoon in the sun and warm up a bit. It was pretty cold when it first come out of the big main."

"I see," Campbell said. "Then the pool was refilled before noon on Monday. If you turned the water in at two or a little after, the pool would have been full again a little after eleven."

"Yes. Or around eleven-thirty. I didn't notice the time particularly, Mr. Campbell. But it had to be about that time. It was all ready for use again when I knocked off at twelve for lunch. I wouldn't have to look at a watch to tell that. Other way around. When I shut the sluice gate, I said to myself it must be about time to eat. When I got back to the garden house on the way to lunch it was five minutes to twelve."

"And you didn't get the pool too full?"

Ransome stared, as if the words didn't make sense. "Too full? How could I get it too full? You ever been in that pool?"

"No. I've been inside the enclosure."

"You ever notice that orange line? Just one row of orange tile set in the blue tile, in a line all around the pool?"

"At the water line? Yes, I've noticed it."

"Well, that's what it was there for. Mr. Andross was a great one for saving little annoyances. You never had to worry whether you had the water the depth he wanted it. I always kept a weather eye on the water level when it was filling, and when it was within a few inches of the orange line I just stayed right there till it touched, then shut the intake gate. How in time could I ever get it too full? I never let it get above that orange water line in my life."

"What were you doing that afternoon after you'd finished with the pool?"

"Superintending the replanting of some terraces on the other side of the hill. Minute one flower died out we cleared the terrace out and put in another. There was always beds to be dug up and planted to new flowers."

"That took you all afternoon, replanting the terraces?"

"It sure did. That's why I was so late honing the mower blades."

"You didn't go back to the pool again?"

"Why, no. Why should I? I was done with it. I didn't have no time to go back and see how pretty it looked. There was so much to do on that hill I never caught up with it. I was always behind with some thing or other."

"You weren't even any place where you could get sight of it?"

"No. I'd have had to go inside the windbreak to see it. I

didn't have no further business inside the windbreak that day."

"Would anybody on the place familiar with your habits have known you'd do that?"

"Sure. Why not?"

"Then," Campbell said slowly, watching Ransome's expression with intent eyes, "you did not get the pool too full, open the sluice again to drain it back to the orange line, go off and forget you'd left the sluice gate up—so the pool could drain out again, leaving only seven inches for Mr. Andross to dive into and break his skull?"

Ransome sat forward in his chair, his eyes widened and his mouth gaped open. "Wh-whaaat?" He stammered on the word and dragged it out into two syllables. "Where'd you hear a crazy thing like that? Is that the kind of accident that killed him?"

"That's right. Thibault found him about ten o'clock. He was dead when Thibault took him out of the pool. Dr. Wheeler says he couldn't have lived ten minutes after his head hit the concrete."

Ransome's sun-browned face looked as if a coating of gray ash had settled on it. "Why, that's the most foolishest thing I ever heard in my life. It's plumb crazy! That pool was full to the water line the last time I saw it. If it had been emptied down to a depth of seven inches, you think Mr. Andross wouldn't have noticed it the minute he seen it? You think you could walk down the tile to the springboard and not notice that fifteen feet of water had shrunk to inches, even in the moonlight? That's a lie. And it's a bad lie. It ain't a lie anybody could expect to have believed by anybody that knew Mr. Andross, and the pool. Put yourself in his place. You think you could have dived from that board without noticin' that the water was away below the orange water line?"

Campbell said, "I didn't know about the water line. I, thought it was merely an ornamental strip of orange tile. But even so, I knew Wark Andross couldn't have done a fool thing like that."

Ransome's voice sank to a hoarse whisper. "My God, somebody killed him! That's the only answer. Somebody killed him and fixed up all that accident business to cover it. That fine, good man! Somebody *killed* him." Suddenly his voice rose, and his eyes burned with anger. "Who told you all that? Whoever cooked up that ridiculous story is guilty as hell! Besides, they ain't even got no sense. Thinkin' anybody as knew Mr. Andross would believe such a thing!"

Campbell said, "Nobody with your experience and your knowledge of the pool and of the people concerned, no. But it doesn't sound unreasonable to the average person not possessed of that knowledge, Ransome. The doctor didn't question it."

"Doc Wheeler?"

"That's right."

"Then whoever planned Mr. Andross' death was slick enough to put it over, Mr. Campbell. If Doc Wheeler said it was an accident, then he *believes* it was an accident. Doc Wheeler is a straight shooter. But it just couldn't of been no accident! You ask Miss Naomi! She'll tell you no such cockeyed thing could have happened."

"It was Miss Naomi who told me, Ransome. She fully expected me to swallow it without question. She thinks I did swallow it, whole."

The blaze died out of Ransome's eyes again, his weathered face looked pale and thin. "She told you that about me forgettin' the sluice was open, and bein' fired by Thibault?"

"She did."

"Then she's in on it," Ransome whispered, appalled. "She's a wild one, always was. Always wantin' her own way, arguing with Mr. Andross till half the time she *got* her way. Sneakin' out on him when she saw she couldn't bend him. I always thought her best quality was honesty, and now she's wrecked that. I'm struck all of a heap. I don't know what to say. I feel like the world was slidin' right out under my feet, Mr. Campbell. At first, I kind of resented your advertising to get me up here this way, me hoping there'd be a good job in the offing, then realizing you only wanted me to answer questions. But I don't mind now I see how important it was. I'd do anything to help catch the one that killed him, if I never got another job."

"The ad wasn't just a come-on, Ransome. There is a job, just exactly the kind of job the ad indicated. You wouldn't know it, of course, that it is clearly stated in Mr. Andross' will that you can never be discharged from Andross employ, you can only leave it of your own choice. Mr. Andross left you twenty thousand dollars, and you will have charge of the grounds at the Canyon House as long as you live, or as long as you want it."

Ransome sat erect, his eyes filled and his chin quivered. "I might have known he'd do something like that. They never made a better man than Wark Andross. And somebody had to go and kill him! God, I'd like to get my hands on 'em."

"So would I, Ransome. Sooner or later, we will. For the present, I want you to stay home and take it easy, and don't talk—not even to your wife. Just tell her you have another job, starting next Tuesday. Show up at the Canyon House about two o'clock, after the will is read. You already know all that concerns you in it. Your appearance at the Canyon House is going to be a shock to somebody, or I miss my guess."

"What do you want me to do?"

"Just get there about two o'clock, and tell the caretaker you are to have charge of the grounds by Mr. Andross' express desire. I'll be handy to back you up."

Ransome took his hat off his knee and stood up. "I'll be there, Mr. Campbell. I'm almighty happy about the legacy. I'm set for life now, me and my old woman are. Man of my age shouldn't ought to have to go around looking for a job."

"You won't have to go job hunting again, Ransome. Thanks very much. I'll see you Tuesday at the Canyon House."

"Yes, sir." Ransome said a dignified farewell and took himself off.

Campbell went into the outer office to relay to Eilers all he had learned from Ransome.

Eilers said, "Lie Number Two nailed, eh? That gal's going to have herself running around in circles pronto if she doesn't look out."

"She's shielding somebody else," Campbell said. "And she's afraid. Don't ask me what she's afraid of. I don't know. Unless she's afraid she knows too much and somebody might want to shut her mouth, or is merely afraid on general principles. I don't think she was in collusion with Wark's murderer; I think that would be going a little strong, even for Naomi. I may be wrong, though. I've been wrong before, I seem to remember."

Eilers said, "No! You don't mean it." He watched Campbell walk to the rack by the door and reach for his hat. "Where you off to?"

"I'm going out to Bess' apartment. I want to talk to her, and more especially I want to see just how the kid's been living. I fear she isn't going to be very comfortable in her new surroundings for a while, and Naomi isn't going to do anything to make it easier. She won't be any long lost sister to Naomi, you know: she'll only be some unexpected usurper taking half the fortune Naomi thought would be all her own. See you when I come back."

Eilers said, "Okay." He slid a card out of the file on his desk and handed it to Campbell. The card held Bess' address and telephone number. It was part of Eilers' job to get and file all clients' phone numbers and addresses for possible future use.

Campbell pocketed the card, said, "Thanks, kid," and went out of the suite and down the hall.

7

On his way to the south side of the city, Campbell's mind was still on Ransome. The gardener had seemed greatly pleased at news of the legacy. Wark Andross had been a man of open heart and lavish hand, whose secret motto for living might have read, "Anything worth doing at all is worth doing well." To anyone on the outside, making such bequests to servants might seem extravagant. To Wark, it had been a natural thing to do.

Campbell's mind turned to Naomi. Why had she sent everyone out to the Canyon House? In talking to her, he had sensed that she was badly frightened. Had she been afraid of what some of the others might give away? Did she feel that she must meet all possible contingencies in person, lest some of the others bungle the job? Was she afraid of what some of them might learn?

He thought, Maybe she wanted to be alone to cover her tracks, her own—or somebody else's. I wonder if she had any reason for wanting to get rid of Wark? Could she have wanted to marry some chap Wark did not approve of? Afraid he'd cut her out of his will if she persisted?

It wasn't pleasant to think of Naomi as being guilty of her own father's death. Campbell sighed, shoving the problem aside for now, as he drew up before 764, the number on the card Eilers had given him. He found it to be a small, third-rate rooming house, not particularly shabby, but not particularly well kept, either. He stepped out of the coupe and walked up to the door which stood part-way open behind its rusted screen, for coolness, no doubt. Beside the door were the letter boxes of the tenants. The card in Number 112 read Bess Holloway and Nina Taylor.

Campbell walked quietly up the stairs, found Number 112 and knocked on the door. The hall smelled of disinfectant and turnips and stale grease.

Footfalls sounded inside the room, the door swung open, and a girl stood there looking out at him inquiringly, but it was not Bess. She was a tall girl, five feet and nine or ten inches at least, straight and slim and exquisitely formed. Thick, curling chestnut-colored hair swept back from her forehead in a loose pompadour. Her eyes were the color of clear black coffee, flashing eyes that might have seemed bold to one less inclined to read beneath the surface; they held the challenging light, the protective chill and hardness that comes from having to fight the world for a toe hold. She had the bright authentic beauty that needed cosmetic aids, Campbell thought, about as much as Johnny Weismuller needed swimming lessons.

The detective said, "How do you do? I'm looking for Bess Holloway."

"She's not here." Her face was angry, hostile. "She's gone on a buying spree."

"You're Nina Taylor, I'd take it?"

"What's it to you? What do you want here, Mr. Patrick Campbell?"

Campbell said easily, "I see Bess told you about coming to see me."

"She did. I know all about it. She described you accurately;

there couldn't be two men answering that description who'd come looking for my room-mate. What do you want?"

Campbell said, "I'd like to come in, if I may. I think perhaps I'd better talk to you. I didn't know Bess had a room-mate. She didn't mention you, Miss Taylor."

"She probably had no reason to. Surely, come on in, if you want to." Her voice lost some of her hostility, and she moved back from the door to allow him passage into the room. "Sit down, Mr. Campbell. You really *have* a load to take off your feet." A fleeting smile lighted her face. She shut the door and stood leaning her back against it. "But I don't understand why you'd want to talk to me."

"You say she told you all about her conversation with me?"

"Yes. She did. The long lost daddy, the three million bucks, the works. Why?"

"She shouldn't have done that, but it's too late to protest now. When do you expect her back?"

"I wouldn't hazard a guess. I expect she'll be all of two hours spending that five hundred you advanced her. It's entrancing business buying new clothes, you know. And she hasn't had too much opportunity, or the wherewithal, for such indulgence. But whatever you want to say, I'd appreciate it if you hurry along and get it over. I'm afraid she's likely to raise a little hell if she learns I've talked to you."

Campbell said dryly, "I'm beginning to understand why she didn't mention her room-mate, Miss Taylor."

"Are you? You're probably right. I could raise a little hell on my own hook if the occasion warranted."

Campbell grinned in spite of himself. "I don't doubt it. But it might be rather inadvisable to kick up any disturbance at this stage of the game."

"Oh, don't worry. I'm not going to put in my oar—yet."

"I see. But you will later when the time's ripe?"

She gave him a steady, unwinking stare. "Wouldn't you like to know?"

"I would. You could trust me, you know. That's what I'm here for."

She hesitated a minute, then shook her head. "The spot I'm in, I'm not trusting anybody. Get that."

"Keep on talking, and I might." Campbell had been surveying the room covertly, the patched plaster walls, the mended but clean old furniture, a bookcase with a few good books in it and several photographs on top of it. One was a picture of a man, dressed in the style of long ago. Something about it was very familiar. The detective's gaze kept coming back to it. One bright note bloomed in a crimson damask portiere drawn back in thick folds to show a small kitchen beyond.

He heard the girl saying, "It's your business to ask questions, Mr. Campbell. How are you on answers?"

Campbell smiled. "Pretty fair—if I *know* the answers."

"All right, try this one. Do you know what it means to walk the streets looking for work with holes worn through your soles? To come home with wet feet, soaked to the hide, shivering? Did you ever feel your belly hitting your backbone, fed on anything you could get and damned little of that, until your mouth watered at sight of a dirty orange in the gutter, and you'd wait around for a chance to grab it and not get caught in the act? Ever get kicked out of a room not fit for a dog to whelp in, hating its meanness and your own inability to afford anything better? Evicted, because you couldn't hope to pay up the back rent? Did you ever sleep in somebody's back alley basement entrance because you had no other out?"

She stopped talking, and Campbell said, "Not exactly. But I

get the picture. A girl with your looks should have been able to do better than that."

Her laughter had a harsh edge. "Oh, yeah? It sounds corny as hell, mister, but my female pulchritude hasn't been for sale yet. You'd be surprised to know how devilish hard it is to get work when you've been foolishly sheltered by an adoring mother who thought work was not good enough for her child, who left you with too many high-flown ideas, no experience and damned little brains."

Campbell said, "I wouldn't say you lacked brains to any extent."

"Thanks, if that's meant for a compliment. So you get the picture so far? Then suppose you try to get the rest of it. Suppose right in the middle of this dilemma, you run into another girl who's had better luck with jobs and eats. She offers to take you in, shares room and grub with you, you get a little meat on the old bones and she even helps you get a job so you can pay your own freight. Then along comes this other girl's long-lost daddy worth several million bucks. The other girl's damned fool enough to show you his picture out of the paper, and a detective's ad trying to get in touch with her mother."

Campbell said, "Good night! Didn't she know any better than to do that?"

"She didn't. But we haven't got all the picture yet. She shows you this sheet with the clippings on it. How long would it take you to conclude that the chap with the millions must be some relation to her, since it was pasted along with the ad? How long would it take you to figure that she was likely to come in for some heavy dough? Don't you think you'd remember shoes with holes in 'em, wet streets, alleyway basement entrances and hunger gnawing at your belly? Wouldn't you be ready to turn any lousy trick on the blotter to horn in on the heavy dough—even to threatening murder, and probably meaning it?"

"I think I might. Others have done it for less."

"Could you blame any girl too much who did?"

Campbell said slowly, "I guess not."

"Then get out of here and let me run my own damned neck into a noose if I want to, will you? Don't worry! I'll get mine! And if I'm let alone, nobody'll get hurt."

Campbell said gently, "You might be the one who got hurt, you know."

She gave him óne long hard look. Then she said slowly, "I think I can take care of myself. You handle your end of this business, and I'll handle mine." She stepped away from the door and opened it, in blunt dismissal.

Campbell rose, started toward the door, and paused, directly facing her. "It looks as though there isn't anything else I can do at the present, I'm afraid. I suppose nothing I could say would have the least influence on you?"

"Not a damned bit. I'm sticking right here and seeing this through my way. You'd better slide out before Bess gets back." She added unexpectedly, "Please."

Campbell could feel almost tangibly the headlong driving force emanating from her. He said lightly, far more lightly than he felt, "Have it your way. I'll go. But I'll be seeing you."

"I'll bet you will!" Her laughter held the harsh grim note again. "After Bess comes into the money and I glom onto my share. I'll be living right there in the Canyon House with Miss Bess, you know. I'll be there, and nobody this side of hell's going to keep me out."

A little note of admiration crept into Campbell's tone. "I believe you. Then—I'll be seeing you, Miss Taylor."

"I shouldn't wonder. And I'll buy you a drink to show you there's no hard feelings." She gave him a sudden, devilish grin. "I might even buy Bess a drink. Don't stumble down the stairs on your way out."

Campbell chuckled. "Would you by any chance know the definition for hellcat?"

"Never heard the word. Keep your specs clean, Mr. Campbell."

"I'll try. Good afternoon, Miss Taylor."

Halfway down the stairs he paused to look back. He hadn't heard the door close, but it was tightly shut. He went on down to his car, carrying with him a clear picture of the beautiful defiant face, the flashing brown eyes and the curling angry mouth.

She went with him, haunting him like a wraith, as he weaved his way through the heavy traffic back to the parking lot. He thought it would be a long time before he could get her out of his mind. He tried to picture her tramping from office to office, sleeping in basement doorways, and the idea was too unpleasant to pursue. He wondered just what demands she had made on Bess Andross.

When he reached the office, he told Eilers. "Wait till you see the Andross girl's room-mate."

"Slick chick?" inquired Eilers.

Campbell laughed. "You'll have to think up some new ones."

"When do I see her?"

"I wouldn't know, Rick. Possibly never. Maybe soon." He

was amused at the growing skepticism and derision on Eilers' face, as his tow-haired assistant sat listening to his report of the conversation with Bess' room-mate. "I think I'll just call back and check up," he concluded.

He picked up the telephone, called the number Bess had given him, and asked for Bess Holloway. The voice that answered was familiar to his ears. He said, "Hello, Miss Taylor. I asked for Bess Holloway. She isn't back yet?"

"No. I don't expect her for another hour at least."

Campbell said, "When I was there talking to you, there was something I wanted to ask, and forgot. That photograph on the bookcase, of the man with large, rather fierce-looking eyes. You know the one I mean?"

"There's only one picture of a man on the bookcase, the others are all women and kids. What about it?"

"The man is your father, isn't he?"

The laughter over the telephone was not particularly amused. "It wouldn't need a detective to guess that, would it?"

"Probably not. You're practically a feminine duplicate of him, and he'd be a little old to be your brother. The clothes told me that the picture had been taken many years ago. Your father is dead, Miss Taylor?"

"What kind of stall is this?" she countered sharply. "Are you trying to find out whether I was lying when I said Bess was out?"

"I don't know yet," Campbell answered. "I still have only your word for it. You could have her tied up in a closet somewhere, for all I know."

"I could have, but I didn't. That might be a good place for her, after the cash and property are properly transferred. I'll keep it in mind. Good-by, Mr. Campbell." The telephone clicked in his ear. He put it down and turned to Eilers, seeing in his mind's eye the neat card in the letter box, engraved with the name Bess Holloway, and the three words *"and Nina Taylor"* written below by pen.

Eilers asked, "That talk of a murder threat—you think it was so much eyewash? Or bluff?"

"It could have been, Rick, but I don't believe so. I think the Taylor girl very likely threatened to kill Bess if she wouldn't come through with a substantial sum and guarantee her a soft berth for life; I think she meant it, and Bess realized the fact."

"Then why didn't Bess sic you onto the Taylor dame?"

Campbell frowned. "I'd been wondering that myself. There's a perfectly logical answer."

"Such as?"

"Such as Bess having in mind those days the Taylor girl hunted jobs in wet shoes and sneaked oranges out of gutters. If she's her father's daughter, she wouldn't hesitate to promise her money and security and cross off the foolish threats. Wark Andross was a pushover for a hard luck story; God knows how many thousands he's given away to undeserving professional deadbeats. He always said he'd rather throw away money on a hundred worthless panhandlers than to have refused one man who was really down on his luck and deserving of a helping hand. His daughter is probably like him."

Eilers said with a dry grin, "There's Naomi, remember? You can't see her weeping salt tears over rooms not fit for dogs to whelp in and similar inconveniences, can you?"

"Naomi isn't her father's daughter. Except for the trifling accident of birth, there isn't an ounce of Wark Andross in Naomi. She's her mother's daughter from stem to stern."

Eilers said, "I guess there's no argument there. Bess is a second edition of Elizabeth Anne in stature; she even looks a little like Andross, too. Only she's not so handsome by a long shot. You don't think Bess is in any immediate danger from the Taylor gal, then?"

"Not now, Rick. She may have been when they first discussed the legacy, she may be again after the inheritance is in the hands of the legatee—but not now! Of all people, the Taylor girl would be the last one to want any harm to come to Bess until after the will is probated and the cash is handed over."

Eilers said, the skeptical look in his eyes again, "All that talk of holey shoes, oranges in the gutter, and so on, sticks in my craw. A little thick, wouldn't you say? Here in L.A. where all the war plants were booming, jobs were as thick as fleas on a dog, and everybody was making more money than they'd ever seen before?"

Campbell said slowly, "I wouldn't be too sure about that, Rick. California was flooded by people coming in in droves to snap up those jobs. Given a situation like that, there are always a few lost and helpless incompetents driven from pillar to post. Where are you more likely to find poverty and starvation than in a big city lousy with money and money-makers? Remember the doting mother?"

Eilers nodded. "Yeah. That's right. Doting mothers can carry things pretty far. More than one kid has turned out a complete sap by such up-bringing, in spite of society at large and the public educational system." He looked up at Campbell meaningly. "Then again, there's the congenital chiseler, who'd spin that kind of yarn to land a soft seat and easy pickings, and be smooth enough to get away with it. You think she made Bess Andross believe her tale of woe?"

"It's possible, if that's the kind of character she is. I'd be more inclined to think she had been through some heavy sledding, and merely laid it on a little heavy, and Bess could see that and forgive the exaggeration and feel sorry for her."

"Probably kept right on feeling sorry for her even after she realized she was being imposed upon and didn't have the heart to kick her out."

"And there's always the angle that the two girls might have grown fond of each other," Campbell said, "and the Taylor girl didn't reveal her vicious streak until she learned Bess was coming into real money. She'd been having it so easy since Bess took her in, she would make a desperate play to get in on the money, too."

"Yeah. That's a convincing argument." Eilers yawned and got to his feet. "Well, it's getting about that time; I yearn for food. But I can't buy that stuff about her tough and hungry days with jobs on every hand, experience or no experience, Pat. She could have got a job as a domestic, any day. Women who had lost their servants to war plants were crying for 'em. Unless she had some kind of so-called pride that couldn't stand being somebody's maid. And only a dumb cluck would go hungry rather than go into service. Nope, I reject the lean and hungry days. I hold out for the vicious baby looking for a soft spot. You coming along and put on the feed bag?"

"Might as well. Nothing to stick around here for at the moment. Just a minute. Be right with you."

8

Naomi Andross did not wait to drive out to the Canyon House on Tuesday. Campbell called her up Sunday afternoon, and got no answer. He then telephoned Drake Freedon. Freedon said Naomi had left for Flour Gold Canyon that morning, taking Thibault and Grannat with her.

Freedon said, "I wish she hadn't. I wish she'd waited for me. She really is going to sell the Beverly Hills place, you know, Campbell."

"Oh, she is?"

"Yes; she's already got it listed, left a key with the real estate man. As soon as everything's settled, she's going back to New York to live. She always wanted to, but Wark wouldn't listen to it. I wish you'd go out there tonight, Campbell. I'd feel better about the whole set-up if you were on hand."

Campbell said, "Naomi might not like it, Drake."

"I don't care a damn whether she likes it or not. Tell her I hired you and I sent you."

"What's all the rush, if the will isn't to be read till Tuesday?"

"I don't like the way things are shaping up, that's what. I've just learned something that makes me uneasy. If you hadn't called me I'd have called you within another half hour."

Campbell asked, "What's come up?"

74

"Quest telephoned me from Logus only a few minutes ago. He said Naomi had asked him to get me on the wire and let me know she'd arrived at the Canyon House safely, which is decidedly unusual for Naomi. She isn't in the habit of reporting on her movements to anyone. Quest made the crack that he wished the will reading were over and done with; the wait was boring to him, he already knew what was in the will."

"How'd he find out?"

"Wark told him, the day he was drafting the will. He even let Quest read the draft. Mart hinted that there were things about the will that he didn't like, but he didn't say what those things were."

"How many people knew about that will, anyhow, Drake?"

"Oh, I suppose all of them may have some vague idea of the general contents, though they wouldn't know the details. I doubt that the servants know anything about it at all."

Campbell said, "Ransome didn't know."

"Oh, you found Ransome?"

"I did. I told you I would." Campbell repeated the gist of his conversation with Ransome. "I told him to be there Tuesday at two o'clock. But what is there in Quest's being familiar with the terms of the will that's upset you to the point of wanting me to go out to the Canyon House tonight?"

"One paragraph in that will which I hadn't mentioned to you, Campbell. At the time it wasn't important for you to know about it; it's very important that you know now."

"What's the paragraph?"

"Just this: if Naomi should die, and Mary is found, Naomi's share of the estate automatically reverts to Mary. If Mary should be deceased, her share will go to Naomi. But, in the event that both girls shall have died before the reading of the will, it all goes to Martin Quest. There are few men who wouldn't plot murder for seven million dollars, Pat. I wish you'd get out there fast, man."

Campbell said, "Yes—I'd better! I'll see Mary, Bess, rather, and explain it to her."

"Tell her to stay put right there in her apartment, and you can send Eilers in early Tuesday morning to pick her up."

Campbell said, "No. Too risky. Bess is my special charge, and I want her right under my eye till the danger's over. I'll take her with me tonight. Does Quest know that she's been found?"

"I didn't tell him. I don't know how he'd find it out, Campbell. All right, take her along with you, then, But won't she be in more danger there than she would hidden away quietly in her apartment?"

"Not if she obeys orders," Campbell said. "I'll have her under guard with Eilers. Do I understand correctly that both girls will be out of danger as soon as the will is read?"

"Quite. If both girls are alive and on hand when the will is read, each shall receive her share of the estate and the paragraph leaving the sums of their inheritance to Quest becomes null and void."

"What if one should die shortly after the reading?"

"If such an event should take place before the will is probated, and the legatee has not named a beneficiary or legatee to me, her inheritance goes into a trust fund for the blind. It wouldn't do Quest a damned bit of good to make any such move after the will is read."

Campbell breathed a mock groan into the transmitter. "Why in hell do legators insist on incorporating open invitations to murder in their last will and testament?"

"I wonder! I told Wark it was exactly that, a regular mur-

der trap. I couldn't budge him. He said what the hell difference could it make when nobody knew what was in the will.
Then he turns right around and lets Mart Quest read the
draft! He'd as soon have distrusted himself as Quest."

"You're sure that paragraph was in the draft Quest read?"
Campbell asked.

"No. I'm not sure. Wark made several drafts, editing and in-
serting and rearranging before he got a final one to suit him.
The paragraph may *not* have been in the draft Quest read,
but we can't take a chance."

Campbell said, "No. Somebody killed Wark Andross, and I
haven't the slightest doubt that money was the motive. If the
murderer was impelled by a million dollars, he isn't going to
stop at a couple more killings to swell the pot to seven million.
﹒ll right, Drake. I'll round up Bess and Eilers and get going
rig. ᵗ away."

"You aren't going to tell them who Bess is?"

Campbell laughed shortly. "Hardly! My acquaintance with
Quest is on the casual side; even Naomi doesn't know me too
well. The others would barely know who I am, if that. They
don't know Eilers at all. Bess will go along as my secretary;
I'll furnish her with a notebook and pencil, and make use of
her in that capacity if occasion should warrant. Eilers can stick
close and put on an act being sweet on her. It won't be any
trouble for Eilers. He's had lots of practice."

Freedon's voice sounded as if he were smiling. "Okay. I'm
much relieved. I'll feel safer about Naomi, and Mary-Bess, too.
The Canyon House is isolated, you know, a good deal of wild
land around it, all belonging to the estate. Squat yourself right
in the middle of it and hold the fort, Campbell. I'll see you
Tuesday."

"Right." Campbell put down the telephone and went into the living room where Eilers was sitting with a magazine and a bottle of iced beer. He relayed to Eilers Freedon's half of the conversation.

Eilers said, "Nice jobs you pick out for me. Thanks. I thought Bess was kind of cute. It'll be a pleasure."

The sun was low in the western sky when the blue coupe turned up Flour Gold Canyon that late afternoon. The car seat was wide, especially fitted to Campbell's height and bulk, and the three had made the long ride comfortably, the diminutive Bess in the middle. When Campbell had called at the apartment, Bess herself answered the door, and Campbell had asked after Miss Taylor. Bess had said, "Oh, she's gone to a movie. I've gotten a little tired of pictures myself, but Nina goes every Sunday."

Campbell had said it was just as well, and explained that the Andross lawyer wanted them to go out to the Canyon now, but he did not mention the reason for the request nor the paragraph in the will that was bothering Drake Freedon. He cautioned her to remember that she was supposed to be his secretary; he did not want her identity revealed until after the reading of the will. Conversation had held a light level all the way out, carried on mostly between Eilers and Bess, the main object being to further their acquaintance, thus making them feel more at home and at ease with one another. Neither the will nor the Andross family came in for any special discussion.

But now, as they started up the Canyon, Campbell said, "I've been wondering, Bess—did you, or do you, believe Nina's hard luck story of her seamy days? How long have you girls been rooming together?"

Bess said, "She came to live with me nearly five years ago, Mr. Campbell."

Eilers put in, "You'd better get used to saying Pat and Rick. No secretary would keep on calling Pat Mr. Campbell longer than about five minutes."

Bess smiled at him, and went on to answer Campbell's questions. "I not only believe it, Pat; I've checked on it and I know it's true. The poor child had a bad time of it there for a while until she met me."

"Child!" Campbell echoed, with good-humored derision. "You're the one who looks like a child. I'd take Nina to be at least five years older than you are."

"That's because I'm so little. Nina was only fourteen years old when her mother died and left her alone in a big, strange city. She didn't know a soul; they'd come here from Arkansas. What could the poor thing know about taking care of herself? She was only fifteen when I met her in the park that day. I've never been so sorry for anyone in my life. I didn't have much—I should say we didn't have much—and I did have a great deal of responsibility taking care of Mother. But I couldn't leave the poor kid adrift after I'd once heard what she'd been through. I thought she'd be company for Mother while I was away, and I didn't care whether she got a job or not as long as Mother lived. Nina was worth her salt doing little things around the rooms."

"Why didn't you mention Nina when you first came to my office?"

Bess gave the detective a sheepish smile. "I guess I was just too bowled over to think of anything. There wasn't any reason to speak of Nina. She wasn't concerned in any way except for being my friend. And of course I'll take care of her. She won't ever have to worry about getting jobs again."

"So she's twenty now, and you're seven years older."

"Yes. She's almost twenty-one. I'll be twenty-eight in September, and she'll be twenty-one in August . . . Oh! Is that the place?"

Campbell's gaze was on the low, rambling stone house partway up the slope to the right, the remainder of the hill rearing above and beyond it. He said, "That's it. It has to be. There isn't any other house in the canyon. It's a short box canyon, and Wark Andross owned all of it. The property extends clear to the tops of the hills on both sides of the canyon. I got all this information from Drake Freedon when I called him up and asked for directions."

Bess said, "It's beautiful." And Campbell remembered that Naomi disliked it. What was it Thibault had said? That Naomi would burn it down if not allowed to sell? Nomy was taking in too much territory.

They came to a jasmine-covered high wire fence, extending along the private canyon road for a half mile. The gate stood open, a road wound up the hill between tall old royal palms. Campbell turned the coupe up the palm-lined drive, and none of them spoke again until after the car had slowed to a halt before the house.

Bess gestured toward the windows, blazing with the reflection of the sunset sky. Her words made the detective suppress a slight start. She said, "It looks as if it were afire."

Campbell wondered why he was suddenly beginning to feel uneasy about the whole set-up. The house didn't have a lonely air. It reared in solitary grandeur on its solid foundations. Tall eucalyptus trees towered behind the stone structure. The gardens in the foreground presented an informal arrangement of perennials, shrubs and trees harmonious to the brush-clad slopes of the hills. Off to the north tilled fields were visible, a few cattle and horses roamed at pasture. Barely visible was the home of the resident farmer who also doubled as caretaker when none of the family was at the Canyon House. The caretaker and his wife probably would have returned to their own farm house now, Campbell thought.

They got out of the car and went up the steps, and Grannat opened the door, smiling a welcome.

Campbell said, "I think you know Eilers, Grannat; I've brought my secretary, Miss Holloway. We've come to stay till after the will's read, at Mr. Freedon's request. You'll find some bags in the car."

Grannat's smile turned to a sigh of relief. "I'm very glad to know you'll be here, sir. Miss Naomi was saying only a few minutes ago that she was sorry you weren't due till Tuesday."

Campbell asked quickly, "Is anything wrong, Grannat?"

"Well, no, sir, not really." He hesitated, then added confidentially, "But Miss Naomi seems to be worried about something."

Campbell said, "I see. Where is everybody, do you know?"

"Miss Naomi's up in her room, sir, and I believe Mr. and Mrs. Northrup are with her. You'll find Mr. Quest and Mr. Overholt in the living room with Miss Mace and Miss Dunham. Mr. Ireland went for a walk up on the hills this afternoon and hasn't returned yet. If you'd all care to come into the living room, I'll be glad to fetch you a drink. Dinner will be ready in about three quarters of an hour."

"That's fine. We'll take the drink, Grannat. Come along, Bess."

Grannat showed them to the living room, and went away to see about the drinks and having the bags brought in.

Martin Quest got quickly to his feet and came across to greet the detective and his companions, hand outstretched in welcome. Quest was a small man, with a slim, compact and graceful body. His small hands and feet were as finely turned as a woman's. His friends sometimes said jestingly that from the neck down Mart Quest was a Greek statue in miniature, but from the neck up he was a gargoyle. His head was large and almost completely bald. Only the thinnest fringe of brown hair ringed the back of his head, none at all was visible in front. His nose was heavy, his eyes blue and deep-set in his thin ugly face. His scant brows and lashes were almost white, his teeth big and crooked in his wide mouth.

Yet he looked young; something about him was alert and alive. Manifestly, he was somewhere in his early thirties. Five minutes after you met Martin Quest you forgot his ugly face and remembered nothing but his charm.

He said to Campbell, "Welcome to the fold, Pat! I didn't know we were to have the pleasure of your company. And your secretary, Grannat said? Miss Holloway. Glad to see you all. How are you, Eilers?" He turned to the other three people in the room. "Come on over here, folks, and meet the company. This place needed a little livening up."

Campbell watched from the corner of his eye, to see how Bess received the introductions to these people who were meeting her so casually, having no idea of her true identity. She seemed a little abashed and uncomfortable in the big room, but she carried it off well. It was probably the largest room she had ever seen, he thought—Wark's ideas ran to space and height—and she didn't know quite what to do with her hands.

The detective's attention expanded to include Francie Dunham, a little taller than her fiancé, slim and serious and earnest; to Sally Mace, a dark girl of average height and awkward build, a nervous and voluble sort of young woman. Ranny Overholt stood behind the two girls, grinning amiably at nobody and everybody, a strong, toughly built young man with dark red hair and a handsome florid face.

Whatever had upset or worried Naomi, Campbell told himself, had not spread to these four young people here. They were all cheerful, cordial and at ease. Eilers stayed close to Bess; that was to be his job here at Canyon House, and he figured he might as well set the pace for his conduct now.

Ranny Overholt said to Campbell, "I don't know what use we're going to have for a famous detective, but it's another shot of rum in the coffee to see one around. How's the detecting business?"

"Oh, fair. Fair." Campbell returned Overholt's engaging grin. "How's fishing?"

"Might snag a few bass above the dam three or four canyons west. So I hear tell. I've been too lazy to go up and see. I'll leave the tramping to Quent Ireland this trip. He dotes on it."

Grannat came in with a tray of frosty glasses and passed them around. As he went out of the room, Naomi came in through the arched door opening off the stair well. She came straight toward Campbell, followed by an older woman only a little more blond and buxom than Naomi herself, and a thin stooped man with a red face and straggling remnants of gray hair.

Naomi said rather loudly, "Am I glad to see you, Pat! Grannat just told me you'd come. I'd like you to know my Aunt Jewell and Uncle Ike, Mr. and Mrs. Northrup—Mr. Patrick Campbell."

Introductions went around again, and the detective, watching Naomi and Bess greet each other, thought he had never seen two girls look less like daughters of the same man. He wondered whether the air in the canyon were always this cool in the evening, regardless of the heat of the day. Grannat was going around turning on lights. The sunset had faded to quick dusk between the hills, and a damp chill was closing in.

Campbell heard Naomi saying, "I hope you don't mind staying two or three days out in the sticks, Miss Holloway. Some people like the country. They can have my share. This house was only a shell when Dad bought it four years ago, remodeled it and put on the service wing."

The detective found himself listening intently for Bess' reply. Bess said, "Oh, I like the country. I like this place. I think it's grand."

Naomi's answer sounded amused, and slightly dry. "You can have it. I can't get back to town too soon to suit me. No shows, no place to go, nothing to do. Deliver me from such stagnation!"

Quest said, "Don't pay any attention to Nomy, Miss Holloway. She has a depraved taste for the bright lights."

The conversation became general, light and jibing, but under the raillery Campbell sensed a prevailing uneasiness. He saw that Eilers was hovering dutifully around Bess, and he went quietly, unobserved, out of the room into the hall.

The butler came toward him from the back of the house, slowing to a pause as he caught sight of the detective. "Did you want something, Mr. Campbell?"

"Yes. I was looking for you, Grannat. I want you to show me this house from end to end, and don't miss a corner."

"Yes, sir. I'll be very glad to."

The detective found nothing noticeably unusual in the structure. He filed away in memory the general layout of the building and the situation of the rooms and the servants' wing. Grannat showed him the rooms that had been assigned to

Campbell and Eilers, with an adjoining room for Bess. They came in the end to the kitchen, where Sophronia, the cook, the footmen and one of the serving maids, were busy getting the evening meal ready. It occurred to Campbell suddenly that, when he had been talking to Freedon about the terms of the will, no bequest had been mentioned for the cook.

Sophronia, commonly called Phrony, big and black, capable and loyal, had been with the Andross household for a long time, ever since Andross had come to California. It wasn't conceivable that Andross would have made no provision for Phrony along with the other servants, yet Freedon certainly hadn't spoken of any legacy for the Negress. The detective walked over to the stove, where the cook stood heaping fried chicken onto a large serving platter, and she looked up at him with a delighted smile.

"Even', Mistah Campbell! Ain't seen you foh a long time."

Campbell said, "Good evening, Phrony." He glanced at the other three servants, whose attention was for the time being focused on something Grannat was saying to them. The detective lowered his voice. "Phrony, I don't suppose you know what provision Mr. Andross made for you, do you?"

"Deed I does, sah! He sho' was a fine man! I'se black sah and some people don't like black folks. Mistah Andross, he say he wasn't takin' no chances on anybody thinkin' he was leavin' too much to a niggah and tryin' to do me out of it. He was gwine fix things foh me while he was still livin'."

"And did he?"

"He sho' did, sah! He done deed me a li'l house and lot in Los Angeles where I kin live close to my sistah and her fambly—I got it rented now. Then he done fix me up wif a trus' fund that become active on the day he die, so's I get two hundred dollahs a month long as I live. Ain't no niggah-haters gwine do *me* out of my 'heritance, Mistah Campbell. No, sah! Mistah Andross, he sho' was some man!"

Campbell said, "Yes. He was. I might have known he wouldn't forget you, Phrony. Yet, it makes me a little curious, too. Just who in this household is a Negro-hater?"

Sophronia hesitated, then said in a subdued undertone, "Miss Nomy, she don't like black folks much, sah. She done tried to get her daddy to fiah me plenty times. He tol' her to mind her own business. I reckon she's gwine th'ow me out any day, now. I'd sho' like to stay on heah at the Canyon House."

Campbell smiled. "I think I can promise you that you'll stay here as long as you please, and Miss Naomi won't be here. Somebody else gets the Canyon House. You leave that to me."

"Yes, sah!" Sophronia's black face brightened with a pleased and broad smile. "Thank you, sah."

"You really do like the Canyon House, don't you, Phrony? You aren't one of those who yearn for the bright lights, then?"

Sophronia's laughter was deep and faintly deriding. "Miss Nomy can have all the gas fumes and horns blowin' and cars rattlin', sah. I'd like to stay in the Canyon House till I walks wid a cane and grows me a long gray beard."

Campbell laughed, commented that the chicken smelled delicious, crossed the room and went on into the hall with the butler. He asked the same question and received a like answer.

"Would I mind staying on at the Canyon House permanently, sir?" Grannat's eyes warmed, and his smile was quick with pleased surprise. "I'd like it more than I can say. Mr. Andross and I were of the same mind about the country, sir. Am I supposed to go with the Canyon House?"

"I have a hunch it's going to turn out that way, Grannat. I'm awfully glad you don't mind."

"Mind, sir! I can't think of anything I'd like better."

Campbell said, "Well, a few things are shaping up right, anyway, Grannat."

"But there's plenty that isn't, sir?"

"I'm afraid so, Grannat."

"You think there's more trouble ahead?"

"There's more trouble brewing, yes. It won't boil over if I can help it. But a man can't always avoid things of that sort, no matter how hard he tries. Somebody doesn't understand, or talks in the wrong place, or refuses to obey orders. And, I'm going to have orders for everybody in the house, Grannat. You included."

"Yes, sir." The old butler looked at him earnestly. "You can depend on me to listen well and obey to the letter, Mr. Campbell."

"I know that, Grannat. This is the first thing I want to see put in order. The business of locking up the house at night. You attend to that, I suppose?"

"Yes, sir. I can promise you that all doors and windows will be promptly secured when the family and guests go to bed."

"Good. And further, I want keys to all the rooms, Grannat. I want to lock everybody into his room, but I don't want them to know I'm doing it. Since I don't know the order of things here at the Canyon House, I want you to tell me the best way to go about it."

Grannat said, "Oh, that will be very simple, sir. The bolts to all the outer doors and windows are quite secure. Since the house is always locked against any intruder, no one ever locks the door to his room. There are several sets of keys to all the doors. Just ask Miss Naomi for a set of keys. She'll be agreeable to anything you want done, and she won't tell the others."

"Thanks, Grannat. I'll just attend to that right now. Go in and tell Miss Naomi that I'd like to see her out here, will you?" Campbell nodded toward the small lounge they had been approaching as they walked.

The butler went in search of Naomi, brought her back from the living room, and went on to the back of the house.

Campbell stood near the side door which opened from the lounge onto the patio. Beyond the patio he could see the big garage, and the wide concrete apron in front of it. He turned quickly as Naomi neared and smiled at her.

"Sorry to bother you so soon, Naomi. But I want a set of keys to all the upstairs rooms." He explained what he had just told Grannat, about locking the doors.

Naomi said curiously, "Why the dickens don't you just tell them to do their own locking?"

Campbell shook his head, still smiling. "I told you I don't want them to know that their doors are locked. I have my reasons. Let it go at that, will you?"

Naomi shrugged, her interest in the odd request already dissipated. "Anything you say, Pat. Sounds funny, but it's okay with me."

Campbell said, "It's going to sound even funnier. I want their own keys to the doors taken out and laid handy in plain sight, on a bureau or dresser. I will trust you to lock your own door. I don't think you'll fail me. And I want you to promise me not to open your door for anybody but me. If anyone tries to get at your windows, yell like hell. I'll be patrolling the hall."

Naomi sobered instantly, all levity and light mockery fading from face and eyes. "You aren't trying to frighten me?"

Campbell said dryly, "Not any more than you are already frightened, Nomy. Skip it. Get me the keys, will you?"

"Of course. And I give you my word to say nothing to anyone, to lock my own door, and not open it for anyone but you. How long is this sort of tight guard going to be held on us?"

"Till the will is read, Naomi."

She turned away without another word, and went down the hall toward the stairs. The detective stood waiting by the side door, gazing through the window out beyond the patio and the garage at the hills. In a few moments the girl returned, and held out to him a bunch of keys on a ring.

"Here you are, Pat. I suppose you wouldn't tell me what this key rigmarole is for?"

"Of course I'll tell you. I want everybody to go to his room with the idea that he's an absolutely free agent. I want him to keep that idea. I'm going to have the lights out and the hall dark. I'd rather no one hears me or knows I am there."

Naomi said suddenly, "I get it. If anybody gets a roaming foot, you want him to be able to get out of his room, but not without making sufficient noise to attract your attention."

Campbell smiled and nodded as he slipped the ring of keys into his pocket. "You've got it. And if anybody does do any roaming about, I want to know what door he comes out of."

She didn't ask the obvious question, about the threat of danger to herself, about there being a probable killer in the house. She did not mention her father. She gave Campbell one long, hard look, and turned away, went out of the small lounge and back to the living room to her guests.

Campbell remained where he was, gazing out the window

toward the hills, thinking. The girl knew well enough that she was in danger. Her failure to ask those questions proved that clearly enough. Still, she would have needed to be far less intelligent than she was not to realize his meaning—when he had told her to open her door to no one but him, to scream for help if anyone tampered with her window.

He sighed and walked slowly out of the lounge, making his way toward the room where the others were gathered.

Quentin Ireland had come in while the detective was talking with Grannat and Naomi. Campbell labeled Ireland a brown man; a man with skin burned deep brown by the sun, with brown hair and brown eyes. He was even dressed in brown. He was a thin man, a shade above six feet in height, with a kind of restless, wolfish air about him. He was paying very absorbed attention to Naomi. Campbell thought, So, that's why he's here—I wondered. He thought, too, that Naomi didn't seem to return any part of Ireland's rather pathetic devotion.

He glanced around the room, gauging faces and temperaments. They're all here, he thought. Friends, relatives, and a killer. Wark Andross' killer. And Naomi knows it as well as I. But—he isn't wearing any label. She probably realizes that, too.

9

THE LATE AFTERNOON FADED to night, they all went in to dinner, and the hour was still early when they separated to go to their rooms. The detective took up his station in the hall, turned out the small light left burning at the head of the stairs, and paced slowly up and down. One by one, he checked off the rooms and their occupants, a time or two he turned his pencil flash on his wrist watch. Everyone was in his room with the door closed by nine-thirty.

Evidently the Northrups had undressed and gone right to bed. They had turned out their lights and were quarreling. Jewell's voice was loud and angry; Ike's was defensive and nearly as loud. Campbell grinned to himself and locked their door. They were both talking at once and he couldn't distinguish a word.

Ireland was very quiet in his single room, but his light was on. Campbell finally caught the sound of whispering pages, and knew that the man was reading. Shortly afterward, the bath was turned on in Ireland's room and Ireland began to sing in the tub. Campbell locked Ireland's door while the singing was lusty. He glanced at his watch, the time was 10:05 now.

Francie Dunham and Sally Mace were giggling and chattering, and the detective heard them laughing loudly at Francie's imitation of Cass Daly. As long as they were snickering and shouting in mirth, he could know they were there. He wouldn't hurry about locking their door. They were the ones most likely to take a sudden idea to go downstairs on some probably silly but equally innocent errand.

It was very quiet in Overholt's and Quest's room, he noticed. He managed to catch what sounded like the slapping of cards a time or two, and some muttered words that did not carry. He thought they might be playing rummy or something of the sort. He decided to go in to talk with Eilers for a while. The time was 10:15 when he turned into his own suite.

He told Eilers how the occupants of the rooms were occupied, got himself a drink, and went back to patrolling the hall at 10:40.

The girls were still giggling. The Northrups had ceased their quarreling. Naomi's light was on but there was no sound from her room. Ireland had gone to bed and turned out his lamp. Campbell went on to Quest's door. Quest and Overholt were talking now. They were making enough noise to cover any slight click of the lock. As the detective turned the key in their door the big clock downstairs chimed eleven.

Campbell stepped back in his own room for a moment to go to the lavatory, exchanged a few remarks with Eilers and returned to the hall. Sally was reading aloud to Francie, now; from the few words he caught it sounded like the kind of poetry to appeal to young girls. All the other rooms were quiet. Sally's reading was a rather pleasant sound. Under cover of that sound, he moved on past their door.

At eleven-twenty-five Campbell stopped before Naomi's door. Sally's voice carried clearly through the still night air, and maybe Naomi was no lover of poetry.

Campbell tapped on the door. "Anything bothering you, Nomy?"

"Is that you, Pat?"

"That's right. Can't you get to sleep?"

"Nothing's bothering me. I was just thinking, that's all."

Campbell said okay. He returned to his suite and told Eilers everybody had about settled down.

Eilers said, "The girls finally pipe down?"

Campbell chuckled. "They're reading poetry, now." He glanced at the connecting door, behind which Bess was settled in her quarters, all openings into her room securely locked and bolted with the exception of this connecting door. "Bess get to sleep all right?"

"I guess so. I haven't heard a peep out of her."

Campbell glanced at his watch. The hour was nearing midnight. He took the keys out of his pocket and tossed them into Eilers' lap. "Take care of these for the time being, kid. It's getting about time for somebody to make a move, if he has anything planned for tonight. I might be called away from the hall. I want you to be able to get into any of the rooms if I shouldn't be around and you should hear anything suspicious going on."

Eilers said, "Check," and pocketed the keys.

"Everybody's key is on his bureau in plain sight, if someone should want to get out. If you hear anyone fumbling with a knob, then unlocking a door, pull on the light in front of our door, see who it is and what he's up to. Don't take chances on missing anybody who might start to prowl, if I shouldn't be around." Campbell yawned. "Guess I'll go check on the girls."

Out in the hall, he reached the door to the girls' room in time to hear Francie say, "Don't you think we've had enough poetry for one night?"

Sally said, "Yes, I do. Let's go to bed." He heard a book slammed shut. He swore at his own absentmindedness, and went back to his own room.

He said to Eilers, "Give me those keys back. I forgot I hadn't locked the girls in."

Eilers tossed the keys to him. "Quest has the best money motive."

Campbell said, "Looks like it. But why would anyone want to kill Wark, kid? Did any of them have a real motive? They were all welcome in his house, they lacked for nothing."

"Maybe somebody just got tired of waiting. If I knew I was coming into real dough, I might get tired of waiting and wish to hell I had it while I was still young enough to get some fun out of it. A hundred thousand bucks or over is a lot of dough in any man's language."

Campbell said, "That won't wash, and you know it. Somebody had a more urgent motive than merely being tired of waiting. There are two things I want to know: I want to know what Wark was doing that hour or more after he'd gone out to the pool, and before he was killed. And I want to know who pulled up the sluice gate and emptied the pool the second time."

"You haven't smelled out any leads yet?"

"Nary a scent." Campbell sat down on a chair near the door. "You haven't heard any significant remarks anywhere to pass along?"

"Nope. Not a thing, Pat. I haven't had much chance—sticking so close to Bess, you know."

"Yes, I know. How was she feeling about everything when you last talked with her?"

Eilers smiled faintly. "Sleepy, and more than a little awed by her surroundings. Trying like hell to act as if she'd always been used to the plush and not doing a good job of it. I coached her off and on. She learns quickly."

"Did she say how she liked Naomi?"

"Never even mentioned her." Eilers emitted a subdued chuckle. "But she was watching her closely all evening—on the sly—and trying to act like her. She'll get along."

Campbell said, "I fancy. Well, I'll have to check up on folks, Rick. So far, all avenues are blind alleys. And there are so many things I want to know about so many people in this house."

"How are you going to find out?"

"Well, I won't find out sitting around here on my el fideldo and gassing with you, bucko." Campbell rose from his chair and started out of the room. "Keep your ears open and your eyes peeled, and don't let Morpheus get the drop on you." The detective glanced at his wrist watch. "It's nearly midnight. I'm going on a still hunt. Telling Bess and Naomi to lock and bolt all doors and windows and not step out of their rooms isn't enough; I want to see whether I can catch anyone trying to gain entrance to either room."

Eilers said, "Hell! Nobody knows who Bess is!"

Campbell smiled thinly. "I wouldn't want to risk a very big bet that somebody might not make a shrewd guess as to her identity. Wark let two people in on the secret of his elder daughter's existence; Drake Freedon and Martin Quest. I have a secret; you're my best friend, so I tell you; you have another best friend, and you tell him; he has a best friend of his own—"

Eilers said, "Ring around the rosy; you can save your breath."

"And our murderer isn't going around handing out information," the detective pursued dryly. "Everybody in this house may know of Mary Elizabeth Andross' existence for all you and I are aware. About the only person I'd feel halfway sure is still in ignorance on that subject is Naomi. I wish that girl would call it a day and get to sleep. The last time I slipped down the hall to take a look, about ten minutes ago, there was still a crack of light under her door."

"Maybe she's gone to sleep and left the light on."

"Oh, no she hasn't. I tapped on the door and asked her if there was anything bothering her that she couldn't get to sleep. She said she was just thinking."

Eilers said, "Deplorable habit. Breeds insomnia."

"You can say that again." Campbell walked over to Bess' door, stood listening an instant, and heard nothing. "Seems to be sleeping peacefully, eh?"

Eilers said, "Yep," and Campbell went out into the hall, leaving his assistant seemingly half asleep in his chair, but actually very much on the alert and with a gun in his pocket.

The detective walked down to Naomi's door, to find that her light was out and the door locked. Francie and Sally were still talking, but they were saying their good nights and had also turned out their lights, so he knew they were in bed. He turned the key in their lock while they were indulging in a last giggle over something, stepped back into his room long enough to return the key ring to Eilers, then resumed his quiet patrolling.

The big house was very still now, save for the old clock downstairs, just striking the hour of midnight. After the last peal of the clock's gong died away, the stillness seemed doubly profound. Out in the eucalyptus trees a mockingbird whistled and trilled. Down the hall behind some closed door a broken snore sputtered as breath was exhaled through loose lips.

The rooms were all numbered in Spanish, in letters two inches high, sterling silver against the dark oak casing above each door.

Campbell had the occupants of the rooms solidly in mind.

At the far end of the hall in *Cinco,* Martin Quest shared one of the suites with Ranny Overholt. Next to Overholt and Quest, in *Tres,* were Ike and Jewell Northrup, in a single room with bath attached. At the head of the stairs on the same side of the hall, in *Uno,* the largest of the three suites, Naomi had her quarters. This was, as it would be for Naomi, the finest and most luxurious of the sleeping rooms.

Across the hall from Quest and Overholt, in *Seis,* another single and bath, was Quentin Ireland. Across from the Northrups was *Quatro,* the suite in which Campbell and Eilers had Bess under watchful eyes. The last single room, *Dos,* across from Naomi, Francie Dunham shared with Sally Mace. All the rooms were large, the doors many feet apart, the hall long.

Campbell tabulated the position of each occupant in relation to the others, as a poker player reviews the cards he holds. Then he walked on toward the head of the stairs. The Canyon House had its own light plant and the current was strong. If there were a light on in any room he would be able to detect it at the door. None was on.

He stood still for a moment again, listening intently. Nothing greeted his ears in any direction but silence. Apparently, everyone had gone to sleep.

He turned back down the hall, moving slowly and noiselessly on the thick carpet, conscious again of the chill and dankness in the air. He discovered that it was one of the Northrups who was doing the snoring. He remembered with an involuntary smile that Rick Eilers called that kind of snorer a bubble-blower.

He began his patrol on the return lap toward the head of the stairs. He tried each door as he passed, and found them all locked. This should have made him easier in his mind.

Apparently nobody had discovered the locked doors, nobody had used the key off the bureau and opened a door when his back was turned. Unless they'd done so, then been smart enough not to leave the door unlocked. But he was uneasy. The chill had strengthened to downright cold in the canyon; to the dankness was added the musty odor of buildings that are closed and unused for long periods at a time. The stillness and isolation of the country, which Naomi disliked so much, closed in on him. He walked on, listening. He thought once that some other sound alien to the snore and the mockingbird's song had caught his ear, but it had been faint, quickly dissipated, if indeed he had heard it at all.

But now as he reached the head of the stairs, the snoring had abruptly stopped, the mockingbird ceased singing or flew away from the eucalyptus trees, and the detective became aware of the alien sound again. He had not imagined it; it was the kind of sound to make his nerves crawl, rising from somewhere below him on the stairs or near the foot of the stairs—the painful, rasping intake of breath, scarcely more than a gasp.

Campbell turned on the pencil flashlight he was carrying and started swiftly down the treads, playing the concentrated bright beam ahead of him. Then his hurried pace slowed. He had never been sorry that he had, long years ago, deserted the medical profession to become a private detective. He had been thankful countless times for the advantage of that remembered training and had always continued to keep abreast of the modern advance of pathology. He was grimly grateful for all his technical knowledge now, as he stared at the spot where the flash beam ended in a pool of radiance.

Lying on the carpet at the foot of the stairs, her face drained of color, her eyes straining frantically up at him, Naomi An-

dross was fighting for breath with all the will and consciousness still at her command.

The detective took the remaining stair treads in one long
leap and bent over her. There was a small spot of blood, almost black in the flash beam, on the breast of her white satin-
and-lace negligée. He reached down with his left hand and
pulled aside negligée and nightgown. The wound on her
breast would have been almost undetectable but for the slight
smear of blood. She had been deeply stabbed with some
strong, round instrument, some sort of long prong, no kind
of common weapon he could call to mind—too thick for an
ice pick.

Campbell poked the pencil-flash into his mouth, holding it
in place with his teeth, bent and lifted the girl carefully in his
arms. She was a big girl, but he was a much bigger man; he
carried her easily, lightly, up the stairs and down the hall to
Quatro. He kicked softly on the door, three times, and almost before the muted thud died in the stillness the door
swung open.

Eilers said, "Heard you coming," and backed out of the
way.

The detective stopped when he reached the wide bed and
laid the girl down gently. The gasping breath had not
changed, her gaze was still held straining on his face. Eilers
stood motionless, awaiting developments or orders.

Campbell said to the girl, "Why in God's name did you
come out of your room after promising me not to?"

"But you—called me." Her voice rasped, difficult, thick. "At
least—I thought—was you. Know better—now."

"When?"

"Ten-twenty. I looked."

Campbell glanced at his watch again, it was now twelve-ten. He took hold of her wrist and held his fingertips against her pulse.

Naomi gasped, "Get doctor—quick."

The detective said quietly, "I'm a doctor, Nomy; that is, I was once. I can take care of you. Rick, get her a glass of water. Listen, Naomi, don't try to do much talking. I'll ask you what I want to know, just answer yes or no. Somebody called you at ten-twenty and pretended to be me. Did he *say* this is Pat, Nomy, or something of the sort?"

"Yes—Pat, Nomy—come on out."

"You put on your negligée and came out. There were no lights on anywhere, of course. He didn't want to be seen."

"No."

"Was he waiting for you by your door?"

"No."

"He'd gone on somewhere. Where? Down the stairs?"

"Yes."

"I see. And he called again, and you followed down the stairs, still thinking it was I."

"Yes."

"Then what happened? Use as few words as possible?"

"Nothing. Somebody grabbed me—around shoulders—something stuck me—in chest—hurt, horrible. I fell down. That's all."

Eilers put a glass of water in his hand and Campbell bent to lift the girl's head and hold the glass to her lips. She took one small swallow, with difficulty. Campbell let her head down to the pillow and handed the glass back to Eilers, shaking his head meaningfully at his waiting assistant.

He said to the girl, "You haven't the slightest idea who decoyed you down the stairs and stabbed you?"

"No." The word was barely audible. The gasping breath

had become a bit more stertorous. Campbell said nothing, but stood there holding the girl's hand, looking down at her. She suddenly made a tremendous effort, her voice rose a little, her enunciation became clearer. "Pat. Listen. You have to know. Dad—was murdered."

Campbell said, "I know. I've known it all the time. You've known it all the time, too, haven't you?"

"Yes."

"But you were afraid to talk; afraid of what might happen to you if you did talk. So you tried to cover it, and got your stories all balled up, hardly knowing what you were saying from one minute till the next, half scared out of your wits."

"Yes. Listen. All that time—Thibault thought—Dad was swimming." Her words abruptly came faster, steadier, with an erratic small rush of strength. "He was talking to somebody, quarreling; I went out there—past the pool—I heard him arguing angrily with three people." She stopped talking, as if to hoard her breath. Then she said three names, distinctly. "Mart—Ranny—Quent." Her voice faded to nothing.

Campbell waited, still holding her hand, his gaze fixed on hers. She made one last effort, but it was of no avail. Articulation was no longer within her control. Her eyelids drooped half shut, her irises glazed. The rasping gasp ceased, the heaving chest stilled. Campbell laid her hand gently upon her breast. He looked at his wrist watch. The dial said twelve-twenty-seven.

Eilers said quietly, "Gone?"

The detective turned to confront him. "Yes. We can't always be kind. Nothing on earth could have saved her. She'd been lying there nearly two hours. She was bleeding internally. I had to learn everything she could tell me while she was still able to speak. Go look in on Bess."

Eilers went to the connecting door between the rooms which was closed but not locked or bolted. He opened the door, turned his flashlight into the room, then closed the door and came back to Campbell. "All quiet. Sleeping like a baby."

Campbell said, "Who in this house is a clever enough mimic to imitate my voice and fool Naomi, to ape her voice and deceive me? Who was out of his room at ten-twenty, decoyed her down the stairs, stabbed her, came back to her room and stayed there with the lights on to answer me when I checked, to keep me satisfied that she was safe in her room? To keep me patrolling the hall intermittently until he thought he could be sure she was dead before he turned out her lights, locked her door and ducked back to his own quarters?"

"The case before the court," Eilers said.

"Right. And with a bird as canny as this one, dusting for fingerprints is a useless waste of time—but you can get out your kit and go take a look."

"I'm practically there. And you?"

The detective's jaw was squared, hard; there was a thin white line of anger rimming his set lips. "I'm going to play a damned dirty trick on somebody: not on Nomy, she won't care. She'd approve, if she could watch what goes on. Nobody in this house besides you and me can possibly know she is dead. Only one person knows that something did happen to her; I'm going to worry the pants off him."

Eilers grinned crookedly. "It always gives me a kick to see you go into action. Where to?"

Campbell said, "I'm taking Naomi to Rupe Traid."

The big detective had acquaintances and friends scattered over half the state of California, mainly because he had fostered such acquaintances among doctors, coroners, state police and city police. He kept these friendships alive and active, never knowing when they might be immeasurably important to his activities. That circle of acquaintances included Rupert Traid and George Landis. Traid was a small stout man with gray hair and shrewd blue eyes, licensed physician and county coroner in the small town of Logus several miles southwest of Flour Gold Canyon. Landis was a short broad man with a lean waist and great, powerful hands; his narrow mustache, thick brows and heavy hair were all one shade of tow. He was a state policeman who lived within a few miles of Logus.

Campbell said, "I'm taking Naomi to Rupert Traid, and giving him a full report. Then I'm going on and rouse George Landis out of bed and report to him. I'm telling both of them to keep the lid on tight and give me free rein; all I want is thirty-six hours and fifteen minutes as of now."

"Until the will is read," Eilers said.

"That's right. I'm going to ask George to slip up to the Canyon and stick around under cover over there in the thick scrub beyond the pump house. You've noticed the pump house—little green building with a red roof?"

"I saw the green shack, yes; didn't know what it was."

"You know now, kid. When I get all that done, I'll slip back here and up to this room before daybreak. Tomorrow I'll—I mean later today, it's already Monday, isn't it?—I'll give out that Naomi's gone back to L.A."

"The murderer will know it's a lie, chum."

"Not when I get through with my little yarn, he won't. Then we'll let him sweat. If I can worry him enough, maybe he'll sweat himself right into the gas chamber. Wait till I'm gone before you give Naomi's room the once-over. Lock this door when you leave and be as quick as you can, so as not to leave Bess alone in the suite any longer than is absolutely necessary. Check on her the first thing when you come back."

Eilers said, "Contents fully noted. Will do."

Campbell went over to the bed and lifted the dead girl into his arms. Eilers waited until Campbell was almost to the door, then he switched off the lights and swung the door wide. Campbell went out and down the carpeted hall soundlessly. Eilers closed the door and turned the lights back on. He locked the door, went into the dark bathroom, and stood by the window, looking down at the garage. He could see the front of the garage and part of the concrete apron.

Campbell went noiselessly down the stairs and on to the front door. He reached his right hand out under the girl's body, drew back the bolt from the door, opened it softly and set the lock on night-latch. He closed the door without making any noise, crossed the porch and went down the front steps.

All the way to the garage he kept carefully close to the trees. There had been a minor thunderstorm back in the hills late in the evening, and a thick high fog obscured the sky. The vault overhead was a dim, characterless blue-gray, there was little light anywhere, but he took no chances of attracting the attention of any watchful eye save Eilers'. He had to take one risk when he reached the garage. He laid the girl's body down on the grass, slipped quickly up to the sliding doors, hugging the wall of the garage, and raised the roll-door slowly on its well-oiled mechanism.

He went into the garage to his blue coupe, released the hand brake and put the gear into neutral. He pushed the car out onto the apron, pulled down the garage door, then walked along by the coupe, keeping it in motion, one hand on the steering wheel. At the spot where he had left Naomi's body he stopped the car, lifted the girl to the seat and put the car into motion again.

Like slowly advancing shadows, man and dark car moved down the drive to the Andross' private road, turned into the road and continued the same ghostly progress until the road described a bend around the jut of a hill and the Canyon House had passed from view. Then Campbell got into the car, turned on the ignition, drove slowly for another mile without lights; he switched on the car lamps then, and sent the speed-ometer up to a steadily held fifty miles per hour.

10

Rupert Traid stood looking down at the girl's body stretched on the glass trestle-table, listening to the detective's low, rapid speech. When Campbell had finished his report Traid looked up with a puzzled frown. "You know what it looks like the work of?"

"One of those old-fashioned long hat pins," Campbell answered, "only I doubt they ever made one with so thick a shank."

Traid shook his head. "Funny kind of instrument to kill a girl with, ain't it? Well, you can depend on my co-operation, Campbell. Miss Andross went to L.A. hours ago for all anybody'll find out from me till you give me the all clear. I hope you get him before he kills anybody else."

Campbell said, "I hope so too, Rupe. Be seeing you." He went out of the undertaker's morgue room and got into his car.

A few minutes later he was talking the case over with George Landis. Landis said, "I'll go out with you right now, Campbell. Surest way to reach that scrub by the pump house unobserved."

On the way back to the Canyon, the detective and the state policeman discussed the case. Campbell told Landis what he and Eilers had been able to learn so far.

Landis said, "Well, I'm no detective, Campbell; I don't believe I'd want to be. I'm just a state cop. I'll stand by and be the arm of the law ready to reach and grab for you, but I don't envy you your job. They sound like a bunch of pretty slick articles to me. The way it stands, from the motive angle, looks like Mart Quest's your man, doesn't it?"

Campbell stared at the road ahead, as they passed Logus and swerved toward the foothills. "He has the greatest motive, at least, George. But a hundred thousand to Francie Dunham or Ranny Overholt, or five hundred thousand to the Northrups, might look as big as several million would to Mart Quest. Could be."

"You wouldn't put it past the Andross girl you dug up, this Bess, to like the idea of six million better than three, in regard to Miss Naomi's murder—or, would you?"

Campbell said bluntly, "I wouldn't put anything past anybody with six million bucks in the scales, George. But Bess was right there under Eilers' eye in the next room all the time, and mine part of the time, while somebody was luring Naomi into the hall and jabbing that sticker in her. All doors and windows into the suite were locked, except the door connecting Bess' room to ours, and Eilers still has the keys in his pocket. She'd either have to come through our room to get out, or ask for the key. She couldn't have done Naomi in, which is the only reason she isn't a suspect."

"Haven't I heard somewhere," Landis offered with a dry grin, "that the fellow who couldn't possibly have done it is the one to nail for the crime?"

Campbell gave him a faint answering smile. "Except when you mean the one who really *couldn't* have done it. That's Bess Andross."

Landis yawned. "Well, I sure wish you luck. What are you slowing down for?"

"That's Flour Gold Canyon just ahead. I thought I saw a car coming out of it. Guess I was mistaken. But I saw a light of some kind. Nobody else lives in that canyon. I wonder who's prowling around?"

The light did not show again, as the blue coupe sped on along the road and up the canyon. At the bend in the road where Campbell had turned on the lights when he was coming out, he now turned them off, then the coupe crept along without lights for a way. The detective stopped the car, leaving the gear in neutral, and he and Landis pushed it up the road and the driveway to the Andross garage. Campbell rolled up the garage door, they put the coupe inside, then pushed Naomi's car out onto the apron before closing down the garage door. Then they pushed Naomi's car down to the road, Campbell with one hand on the steering wheel most of the time, and down the road to a small side gully that was heavily wooded by the native scrub. In this gully, fifty feet from the road, they left Naomi's car, completely covered by the scrub and undetectable five feet away.

As they returned to the road, Campbell's flashlight followed the car's trail, and every trace of the car's passage from the highway to the gully was obliterated by the two men before they turned their steps back to the Canyon House. The detective walked with Landis to the tree growth back of the pump house, and returned to the suite of rooms he was sharing with Eilers and Bess, snapping back the night-latch on the front door and shooting the bolt home as it had been before he went out.

Eilers was sitting in a chair by the connecting door, reading a magazine, and he looked up with an inquiring smile as Campbell came into the room.

Campbell asked, "Any luck, kid?"

Eilers grinned. "Yeah. Perfect prints on the outside door-knob—yours."

Campbell said, "The hell!" and sat down on the foot of the bed.

"Prints inside, plenty of 'em," Eilers went on. "Three women and one man: probably Naomi's, one of the maids', and the Northrups'; Jewell and Ike were in the suite with Naomi when we came."

Campbell said, "All quiet?"

Eilers nodded. "I didn't hear a sound all the time you were gone—I mean the wrong kind of sound. Looked in on Bess several times. She's still sleeping like a sloth on a busman's holiday. How'd everything go? You see Rupe and George?"

Campbell said yes, and told Eilers what he and Landis had done with Naomi's car, and that the state policeman was already stationed out by the pump house. "And now," Campbell said, "to wait till the family gets a yen for breakfast. It won't be too long." He nodded toward the window. Through the pane the crest of the hills across the canyon was visible, and above the hilltops the sky was growing light. "Behind one of these doors somewhere," he added, "somebody is waiting for a body to be found and for you and me to howl murder. I hope he, or she, gets a shock that'll trip him, or her."

Eilers frowned. "You think he can possibly be made to believe he didn't kill her?"

Campbell said, "I hope I can make him believe it. As soon as Bess stirs, I want a word with her before we go down."

Eilers glanced toward the closed door behind which Bess lay sleeping. "Kind of a dumb little jerk, isn't she?"

"There's no doubt about that," Campbell answered, kicking off his shoes and lying back on the bed, propping himself on one elbow. "Unless she's putting on an act. I haven't quite made up my mind which it is. People who try to put on an act, especially those who haven't much equipment in the way of brains, can pull some corny attempts at histrionics. They're so dumb it sounds good to them, and how can they realize how it would sound to anybody with a little gray matter in the old skull? She's either putting it on, or she's lying. When it becomes important to know, I'll take her yarn to pieces and find out. Up to now, it hasn't been too important. The only important angle has been that she's Wark's daughter."

Eilers said, "Well, I have thought that she seemed pretty naïve."

"Too damned naïve." The detective laughed shortly. "Pretending she didn't know where Puget Sound was, living here on the coast all her life. Doesn't she ever read a newspaper? No girl who's worked for years in cafés and restaurants could remain such a cow-eyed innocent about people in general and society at large."

"I'd thought of that," Eilers said, leaning forward in his chair, stretching his shoulders and lounging back again. "Waitresses learn the ropes and the answers the hard way. They don't tough it out very long unless they do learn 'em."

"And if she worked in war plants, she'd have had to get her birth certificate, she'd have had to know who she was. Doesn't she suppose I'd realize that, or doesn't she know it herself?"

"What's she lying for?" Eilers wanted to know. "Not to impress you, surely."

Campbell said, "I think she's afraid."

"Afraid of what?"

"Nina Taylor, maybe; that girl's dynamite."

"You think the Taylor dame did threaten her, then?"

"Yes, I think she did. I think she meant it, and Bess fully

realized the fact. That Taylor girl is shrewd, quick-witted. She's resourceful and strong-willed, with a damned forceful personality."

Eilers said, "I'm beginning to get an idea."

"Let's hear it."

"Maybe it's this way: during the time the Taylor girl has lived with Bess, she's hung on like a leech because it was easy pickings, and in order to keep a soft berth with somebody else doing most of the work and bringing in the bacon, she's set herself to control Bess—mentally and by force of character. She's got Bess so thoroughly under her thumb that the poor kid is afraid to say her soul's her own. Buy it?"

"Maybe, kid. I've seen cases like that, where a strong-minded person had a slower-witted one practically hypnotized, and the dumb one didn't even know it."

"Yet, if the Taylor girl really has anything on the ball, why would she force Bess to put on such a front?"

"Not clear yet, kid, to the present sitting. I hate to say it about Wark's long-lost daughter, but you used the right word in the first place; Bess *is* dumb—and dumb enough to be easy prey for a girl like Nina Taylor. What I'm wondering is, how long has the Taylor girl known about those two clippings Anne Elizabeth left with Bess."

Eilers said, "Oh-oh! So maybe the Taylor girl hung onto Bess all this time, merely waiting for the day when Bess might come into real money—and got damned tired of waiting, Pat?"

"Could be. That idea has been crawling around in my skull."

"Tired enough to do something about it? Such as getting into the Beverly Hills place? Draining pools, cracking heads, and whatnot?"

"It's not impossible, Rick."

"Mmm. I don't suppose it is. But if that's your theory, what about Naomi? You don't think the Taylor girl followed Bess out here, do you?"

"I didn't say that was my theory, kid; I said it wasn't impossible as an answer to Wark's death. I don't believe it is the answer. I don't believe Nina Taylor was ever within miles of the Beverly Hills place. I wouldn't be surprised to see her show up here any time, though."

"To keep a close rein on Bess?"

Campbell pursed his lips in a dubious grimace. "I don't think she'd come for any other purpose—in the light of our knowledge at the present time. I'd like to know who was moving in or out of the canyon with a flashlight as George and I were on the way back. I'm fairly positive now that it was a flashlight."

"Well, it wasn't anybody from this house, Pat, unless it was one of the servants. Nobody could have opened a door down this hall without my hearing it. After I got through dusting for prints, I—" Eilers chuckled. "I took steps. Just move outside our door and look up."

Campbell stared at him for a moment in silence, then slid off the bed, walked over to the hall door in his sock feet, and swung the door open. Daylight had been strengthening rapidly as the two had talked, and the detective could now see beyond the open doorway without stepping into the wide hall. A slow grin began to spread across his face, as he looked toward the ceiling, then toward the right and the left.

Again, here was one of those thoughtful things Andross had so often done to spare himself and others minor annoyances. Campbell thought of all the men who had stood in dim halls, groping for doorknobs, fumbling for keyholes, cursing the light switch at the head of the stairs. Wark Andross had thought of them, too, even in the Canyon House. Before every door, from *Uno* to *Seis,* set in the ceiling and trained upon the face of the door below it, was a shaded light furnished with a strong bulb. Each of these lights worked by a pull switch, fitted with a long chain. On the end of each chain hung a ball about the size of a walnut, covered with the same sort of paint that illuminates a watch dial. Coming into the dark hall in the night, the little balls glowed like six dim little stars suspended in the air.

Strung around the Canyon House were numerous objects that were there only because they had pleased Wark Andross by virtue of their rural association. Among these were two or three pairs of silver-mounted spurs, an ancient ox bow, a great iron-tired wagon wheel used as a chandelier, a brightly polished silver horse bell with a clear and penetrating peal, a pair of stirrups, a couple of bronze cow bells—the number of such carefully gathered mementoes decorating the Canyon House would have filled a delivery truck.

The silver horse bell with its sweet and far-reaching tone, its clapper so perfectly hung that the least move of the horse would send that silvery peal calling the bell-mare's followers, had been one of Wark's treasures. It had been hanging in a little ebony standard on the desk in Wark's den downstairs. It was not in that den now. Eilers had fetched and made good use of the silver bell during Campbell's absence.

The door to *Tres,* the Northrups' room, was almost directly across the hall from *Quatro,* the suite Eilers and the detective now occupied. On the end of the chain before the Northrups' door Eilers had tied the silver horse bell. From the chain just above the bell, to the the door of *Tres,* tied snugly to the doorknob, and to the doorknobs of all the other four suites up and down the hall on either side of *Quatro,* ran lines of cord taut enough to show no sway. Except for the door opening into their own suite, no one could have opened any door, however cautiously, without sending the warning peal of the silver horse bell ringing through the night.

Campbell turned back with a grin on his face. "How long did it take you to set up that infernal machine?"

Eilers said, "Oh, about fifteen minutes."

"Well, you'd better take your Rube Goldberg contraption down before the family begins stirring. You might set it up again tonight, though, after the doors are locked."

Eilers said, "Thanks for the compliment. Will do." He left his chair and started into the hall to retrieve the horse bell.

Campbell went back to the bed, yawning. "Compliment, my sternum! That's about the silliest rig I ever laid eyes on."

Eilers said, "Don't be so stingy. You may live to thank me for this rig yet."

Campbell stretched out on the bed and closed his eyes. "It's remotely possible. Hurry up and get that junk down. I hear Bess moving around, and I want to talk to her."

In less time than it had taken him to install his warning bell, Eilers had the strings all in his pocket and the horse bell on the floor under the bed. He hadn't made a sound doing it. He closed the hall door to their suite, went over to the connecting door and rapped on it.

Campbell was thinking that, thanks to Eilers' inventive bent, not only did they know that none of the several guests had left their rooms in the detective's absence; they also knew that no one had returned to the foot of the stairs to make certain Naomi had been killed by the stab. It had been ten-twenty when someone had called Naomi out of her room, pretending to be Campbell. He wondered how many of the occupants of those rooms would have an alibi for ten-twenty.

He heard Bess call in answer to Eilers' knock. "Did you want something, Mr. Campbell?"

Eilers said, "It's me, Eilers. Mr. Campbell wants to speak to you, Bess."

"Oh. Just wait till I put on my robe. I'll be right in."

Eilers returned to his chair. In a few seconds the connecting door opened and Bess came in, leaving the door open behind her. Eilers rose, ushered her to a chair, and again went back to his own.

Campbell sat up on the bed and lowered his feet to the floor. He said, looking at Bess, noting the new quilted robe of dark red, "There are a few points I don't quite understand. I wonder if you'd mind clearing them up for me."

The girl sat with her hands loosely clasped in her lap, watching him. At his words, she shook her head and replied promptly, "Of course not. I'd be glad to tell you anything."

"Thanks. One thing—how could you get a job in a war plant without having your birth certificate?"

Bess glanced at Eilers. He seemed half asleep. She looked back at Campbell. "That was one thing I wasn't going to mention if you didn't ask. It might sound as if my mother were in the habit of being a little tricky, and she wasn't."

"They did tell you you'd have to have one, then, of course."

"Oh, yes. And I went home and told Mother. She said it was impossible to get my birth certificate, and not to ask why. I never had questioned her motives or her truthfulness, I didn't question her then. A girl friend of mine working at the cafeteria said she knew the manager very well and she'd fix it for me."

"And she did fix it?"

"Yes."

"And you believed her?"

"Well, I didn't have any reason to doubt her. I didn't know but what she was a good enough friend of the manager to fix it. I never learned the truth till after I'd left the cafeteria."

"And what was the truth?"

"Well, my mother did get my birth certificate, and she went to see the manager himself, and showed it to him. But it gave my name as that of her former husband, and she didn't want me to know what it was. I supposed then that her former husband must have been my father, and that Mr. Holloway must be my stepfather. Until then, I'd thought Mr. Holloway was my father."

"You didn't say anything to your mother about this?"

"No." Bess shook her head, then sighed, and shifted her small form restlessly in a chair that was too big for her. "I didn't know it till after she was dead."

"Who told you?"

"That girl friend of mine who used to work at the cafeteria. I happened to meet her on the street, and we got to talking, and I told her Mother was dead. Then she said maybe it was all right for me to know about the birth certificate; she thought I should know."

"Who told her?"

"The manager of the cafeteria, Mr. Campbell."

"She didn't tell you the name on the birth certificate?"

"The manager hadn't told her that."

Campbell remained silent for an instant, thinking. Then he said, "I see. And you never found the certificate in your mother's papers after she died?"

"No, and I looked for it, too. I supposed she had destroyed it to keep me from finding out who my real father was."

Campbell said, "And you didn't make the connection between that birth certificate business and the clipping of Wark Andross you were supposed to bring to me?"

"No. Oh, I did think of it, in passing, of course, but it seemed utterly impossible that my father could be the wealthy financier. It seemed fantastic. I wouldn't even let myself consider such a thing until I'd talked to you, Mr. Campbell."

"Why didn't you go talk to the cafeteria manager yourself?"

"Oh, he'd left Los Angeles long before I met my girl friend on the street that day."

Campbell said, "Well, I guess that's all, Bess. I only wanted to get that cleared up. You can go on back to your room. You might as well get a couple more hours' sleep if you can. This household isn't in the habit of breakfasting early. It isn't six o'clock yet."

Bess rose with an air of meek obedience. "Oh, I always get up before six o'clock. I couldn't sleep any more. But I'll have my bath."

Campbell said, "Sounds like a good idea."

The girl returned to her own room. They heard her lock the connecting door and turn on the water in the tub.

Eilers said lowly, "And what kind of rigmarole would you call that?"

Campbell laughed. "A little on the Rube Goldberg side, like your horse bell contraption."

Eilers said, "I think she's just over her depth, Pat—trying to make everything hold together, and not remembering too well what she's already told. No harm in it, probably; there's just something she doesn't want you to find out, and she's none too expert at covering up."

"No argument there, Rick. I'm not ready to make a point

of it, yet. If she's gotten into any unsavory scrapes that she wants to hide, I can't see right now where they'd be of any importance to the main issue."

Eilers said, "I feel kind of sorry for her. It's not going to be easy for her to step into the atmosphere of the Canyon House, more money than she can use, and umpteen servants to eye her like judge and jury."

Campbell sat frowning into space. "I keep thinking of Wark, kid. The last few years, every time I saw him I had an impulse to want to cheer him up. He could never smile wide enough to wipe the set look of sadness off his face. I used to feel that I'd like to drive the habitual bitterness out of his eyes. Life hadn't stacked up to much and he hadn't much use for it. Naomi had failed him, as her mother before her had failed him. And now—I keep thinking about how I always had that feeling of wanting to cheer him up."

"So it doesn't matter so much if Bess is a little dumb, eh? It doesn't matter whether she's stirred up a little pitch that looks pretty black to her limited viewpoint, but which probably doesn't amount to a row of pins. She's still by long odds a better grade of offspring for Wark than Naomi."

"What counts, Rick, is having found Anne Elizabeth's daughter—the girl Wark would have spent half his fortune to find. Some people think the dead can look down and see what goes on after they've left the earth behind. I don't believe it, but that's not saying it couldn't be so. If it is so, it might cheer Wark up now to know that his and Anne Elizabeth's daughter will be here in his house in her rightful place. That's the only consideration I'm pinning any importance on at this stage of the game. First things first, kid."

Eilers made no comment. He watched as the big detective got to his feet and started out of the room. "Where to, Pat?"

Campbell halted and half turned. "This damn key business is getting me down. Hand 'em over, will you? I'd better unlock the doors before people start stirring about. I'd have some undesirable explaining to do if the guests should discover they've been locked in. I'd much rather they didn't know it yet."

Eilers said, "Somebody knows it. Somebody had to use his own key to get out, or Naomi'd still be alive. Hell, who unlocked Naomi's door, Pat?"

"Why, she did, of course. Naomi locked herself in her own room, and promised not to open her door to anyone but me. If she'd kept that promise, made a little effort to be certain it *was* me, you're right—she'd still be alive."

"Somebody must have got a start when *he* tried to come out and found himself temporarily stopped—with his own key right there on the dresser in front of his eyes. Or—could be his door wasn't locked yet when he slipped out." Eilers tossed the keys through the air.

"Yeah? Then he wouldn't have had his key with him, so how did he get back?" Campbell had held out his hand, and the keys landed in his palm with a little unmusical jingle. "Anyway, he got out. He—or she. Every man jack of them was in his room last night, nobody was prowling on the loose for very long, I know that. He must have gone right back to Naomi's room after he killed her, and stayed right there until after he answered me, pretending to be her."

Eilers said, "Somebody besides Bess will have some covering up to do. A locked door he didn't expect, out of his room at ten-twenty, a girl he's sure he killed and it turns out she's not dead."

"If I can make him believe it. I hope he gets enough of a jolt at the breakfast table to give himself away."

The detective went on out of his suite and passed rapidly along the hall, quietly unlocking the door to each room or suite. Within a few moments he returned, to dump an armful of stuff on his bed. Eilers watched without comment as the detective spread out a blue-gray coat. On the coat he laid a blue dress, a small white hat, a white plastic handbag, a pair of white suede shoes and a pair of silk stockings. He rolled the whole into a neat bundle, put the bundle into his own suitcase, locked the suitcase and shoved it back under the bed.

Eilers said, "I suppose that's the outfit Naomi wore to L.A. last night, in case anybody gets curious enough to go to her room and look, eh? I could do with a drink, you know?"

"So could I. Go down and dig up a bottle, will you? Bring up some cigarettes, too. My pack's about empty."

After Eilers returned with the bottle and cigarettes, the two men sat drinking and smoking until Bess came in, dressed and hungry. They went down to the breakfast room to find the table set and Grannat moving about.

Campbell said, "We hoped to find you up, Grannat. Coffee in the offing?"

"Yes, sir. Cook's always prepared for early risers at the Canyon House. Would you like scrambled eggs and ham and toast, sir, or just coffee now?"

Eilers sighed, as he pulled out a chair for Bess and prepared to sit beside her. "We'll take anything that's handy, won't we, Bess? I'm empty to my toes."

Bess said, with a shy, almost frightened side glance at Grannat, "Yes. I'd like eggs and ham—" She hesitated, looking again toward the butler. Eilers said in her ear, "Grannat." Bess said dutifully, "Grannat."

The butler said, "Very good, miss," and went into the kitchen.

Campbell sat down on the other side of Bess. The three of them conversed idly, and the two men ate slowly, with purpose, consuming a good deal of time with their food. The others began to drift in. Ike and Jewell Northrup came before Eilers, Campbell and Bess had half finished their eggs and ham.

Jewell Northrup, stout, blond, and bustling, went toward the other end of the table with Ike's thin figure in tow. Greetings passed back and forth. Jewell said to Eilers that there was another high fog, but she hoped the sun would burn it away early. She added, "I like the sun, don't you, Mr. Eilers?" Her slightly protuberant blue eyes said she wondered just exactly what he and the detective and their little dark secretary were doing there.

Then Martin Quest and Ranny Overholt came into the breakfast room together, followed shortly by Francie Dunham and Sally Mace. Quentin Ireland was the last to arrive, and by that time Campbell and his group were down to a last lingering cup of coffee, and the clock hands were pointing to a quarter of eight.

The butler brought in a tray of tall, colored plastic glasses, and began setting them methodically around at the places without asking whether anyone wanted the contents or not. Campbell glanced at the red glass by Bess' plate, the orange glass by Eilers', the dark blue one with which he himself had been served. It might seem that Grannat was being a trifle careless; he was lifting the glasses with his fingers high toward the rims, handling them with a small thin napkin over his fingers and palm. The detective refrained from glancing at

Eilers, but he knew that his assistant had been holding converse with the old butler, as Eilers would have phrased it.

Jewell Northrup said, "What is this, Grannat? It looks like milk. You know I don't like milk."

"It isn't plain milk, madam. It contains a dash of spice and rum. Very delicate, if I may say so."

Jewell picked up her glass and sniffed of it. She sipped it. "Not bad, if you can stand milk. I can't drink the stuff." She set the glass down and didn't taste any more of the mixture. But all around the table the others began picking up the brightly colored glasses and sipping at the spiked milk.

Grannat set before Eilers a small plate covered by a paper doily. On the doily were crossed toast-sticks. The butler said, "Your dry toast, sir. I hope it's browned to suit you."

"Just right, Grannat. Thanks."

Then the thing Campbell had been waiting for happened.

Jewell Northrup said, "Why in the world is Naomi so late getting down? She's usually the first one scouting for coffee when we're here at the Canyon House."

Francie Dunham glanced down the table, her steady, serious brown eyes faintly puzzled. "I knocked at her door when Sally and I came down, Jewell. I didn't get any answer. She must be sleeping like the dead."

Bess had been sitting silent, with her hands in her lap, her eyes down most of the time, listening dutifully to the conversation. Now she raised her gaze to look at the empty chair beyond Ireland.

An odd, almost uncomfortable silence fell over the room. Some emotion obscurely resembling alarm seemed to communicate itself from one to another. Campbell's veiled glance went from face to face, seeking a set of features wearing the wrong expression. He couldn't find it. Both Mrs. Northrup and

Francie Dunham looked somewhat anxious or troubled. Sally Mace's dark nervous visage held only polite inquiry. Ike's deprecating smile seemed to say, "These women, always fussing over something." Martin Quest's ugly features placidly refused to see anything unusual in Naomi's failure to arrive at the breakfast table at any certain hour or minute. Ranny Overholt was grinning at Ike, winking at some secret jest between them. Only Ireland's thin, faintly wolfish face betrayed the alarm that had seeped into the air.

Campbell said easily, "Naomi went back to Los Angeles last night."

Jewell Northrup said, "What? Well, of all the silly things! What did she do that for?"

Ranny Overholt stopped grinning and looked blank. "Back to Los Angeles? She's nuts! That girl's liable to do anything."

Martin Quest said soberly, "You wouldn't be kidding anybody, would you, Pat? I can't imagine Naomi going ten feet from the Canyon House before that will is read."

Campbell's voice was casual. "Why would I kid about a thing like that, Mart? I'd say she had sufficient reason for getting as far away from the Canyon House as Los Angeles—or farther."

Ireland asked sharply, "Why?"

Campbell said, "Somebody tried to kill her last night."

For a long moment no one said a word. Ike Northrup gasped. Bess flung out one hand and gripped Eilers' arm. He put his hand over hers, clasping it tightly, cautioning her to silence.

Then Francie Dunham gave a faint squeal, as if the detective's words had just penetrated to her intelligence. "Sally! Did you hear what he said? Somebody tried to kill Nomy!"

Overholt shrugged. "Rot! She's always dramatizing herself.

Who in hell would want to kill Naomi? That was just an excuse to get away for the day by herself. She always did hate the Canyon House."

Ireland said tartly, "She hates the country. Not the Canyon House itself, but its isolation in this canyon miles away from any other house, from any town. Hasn't she as much right to her preferences as anybody else?"

Overholt laughed. "Sure! Sure! I can respect other peoples' opinions and prejudices."

Ireland said, "Like hell you can! You're too damned egotistical to grant a right to any opinion but your own. You shut up, Rann; you're too cocky to have much respect for anything."

"Only money," Ike Northrup said. "Ranny has profound respect for the lucre."

No one noticed Grannat, approaching with his tray, the thin small napkin covering his hand again. He began picking up the bright-hued plastic glasses, by the top of the glass as before, arranging them on his tray. No one paid any attention as he walked away.

11

Martin Quest's voice rose, hard with authority, sharp-edged with urgency. "All of you shut up! Give Campbell a chance to talk. What do you suppose he's here for?" Silence went down the table like a little wind, blowing the words away. Quest turned his head quickly, his clear brown eyes fixed on the detective's face. "Did she have any idea *who* tried to kill her, Pat?"

Campbell said blandly, "I don't believe I'll answer that, Mart."

"Well, how did they try to kill her, then? Was she badly hurt?"

Campbell was conscious of all the different faces turned toward him, as he withheld his answer for an instant; Jewell Northrup frankly frightened, Ike frowning and intent, waiting, Francie and Sally both gaping in disbelief, Ranny Overholt openly skeptical and derisive, Ireland white and worried, Quest grim and narrow-eyed. He noticed Bess, too, involuntarily. She looked amazed and excited, but neither frightened nor surprised. Campbell wondered over that for an instant. Then—

The detective said quietly, "Somebody called her out into the hall, pretending to be me. I had told her not to open her door for anyone else. I wonder, did she repeat that to any of you?"

Jewell Northrup's hands, glittering with rings, gripped the edge of the table, her large bust pressed against them. "She told us all, just before we went up to bed. She said for us to do the same, not to open our doors to anyone but you. We promised, but we thought it was silly. We thought she was dramatizing again. We even thought it was silly to have a detective in the house."

Quest said, "It doesn't sound so silly now. Go on, Pat."

"The hall was dark, and whoever called her had gone down the stairs. He called her again, and she followed. At the foot of the stairs somebody tried to stab her with some long-shanked instrument similar to a steel knitting needle filed to a sharp point. It was a well-aimed blow; whoever struck it knew what he was about. He put an arm around Naomi's shoulder, gripping her tightly. She wasn't alarmed. She still thought it was I. Then the would-be murderer struck. He aimed to drive the weapon upward, under the sternum—the breast bone—through the soft tissues into the heart."

Ireland said hoarsely, "My God! Poor Nomy."

Quest's hard accents cut short any further words from Ireland. "Go on, Pat."

"The steel shank—we'll suppose it was steel—missed its path a little."

Ranny Overholt, all his amusement and derision discarded now, asked soberly, "How?"

Campbell said, "Well, Naomi was pretty well padded ever since her kid days. She still is, you know. The weapon went up outside the ribs, into the flesh of the breast. Such a wound would be pretty painful, but scarcely serious. Naomi didn't give him a chance to strike again. She slumped away from his arm and dropped to the floor, pretending to be mortally hurt. The ruse worked. After the fellow went away, and she'd waited to be sure he wasn't coming back, she came up to my room and told me about it. She was determined to leave for Los Angeles without delay. I didn't try to dissuade her. In fact, I helped her."

Francie's voice quivered. "That was awfully good of you, Mr. Campbell. Poor, poor Nomy! Was she suffering much?"

"The pain was entirely gone by the time we left the house," Campbell answered truthfully.

Ireland asked in a flat, emotionless tone, "Was she sure her assailant was a man, Campbell?"

"No. In the dark she couldn't tell. I told her to get dressed, she went to her room and put her clothes on almost in nothing flat, and we went down to the garage."

Ike Northrup said, with a hint of challenge, "We never heard any car go out. And the way that girl races her engine—"

Campbell said, "You couldn't have heard the car; we didn't want anyone to hear. All Naomi wanted was to get away, fast, and leave me to hold the fort. I pushed the car out and ran it on down to the road without lights. Naomi didn't turn on lights or engine till we were far enough from the house for the motor's noise to pass unnoticed. I don't suppose the whole trick took more than an hour. The would-be killer evidently felt certain of his success. Naomi had, of course, left her door unlocked when she went out into the hall, as she thought, in answer to my call. She was too upset and excited to lock it when we went to get the car."

Ranny Overholt said, "What the hell would she lock her door for? Nobody would have any reason to lock his bedroom door here."

"I told her to lock it," Campbell said. "I had reason to think she might be in danger. Either Naomi didn't lock her door, and the assailant used her key, or she did lock her door and took the key with her and he had one of his own. He went into her room and turned on the lights. In this way he hoped to confound me, persuade me she was in her room, and prevent my becoming alarmed at her absence, looking about and finding—as he thought—her corpse. I tapped on the door, the assailant answered, mimicking Naomi's voice as successfully as mine. I was supposed to think Naomi was there. The person inside the room didn't dream she was well on her way to Los Angeles by that time."

Sally Mace demanded shrilly, "Why didn't you go in right then and grab him?"

Campbell smiled at her. "The door was locked, Miss Mace."

Martin Quest looked angry. "You mean you deliberately failed to rouse the house and let him get away from you? You didn't set a watch on the door?"

Campbell's smile lingered, a shade askew. "I'm not sure you'd make a good detective, Mart. Yes, I let him sneak back to his own room, for perfectly good reasons of my own. You needn't worry. I'll get him in my own good time."

Quest said, almost glaring, "I'm not sure I like your methods. Allowing Nomy to go tearing off to L.A., when you should have kept her here and let us fetch a doctor. Not grabbing her assailant when you had the perfect chance."

"Well, no, it wasn't the perfect chance, Mart," the detective contradicted steadily, "for reasons that I shall not at the present divulge. Had it been the perfect chance I would have taken it." He looked from person to person, his gaze lingering, probing. "One of you people sitting at this table tried to kill Naomi Andross last night. I don't suppose there's the slightest chance that the guilty one will admit his identity now and save the others a great deal of unpleasantness, but I'm giving him the opportunity."

He thought grimly, Whoever he—or she—is, he has iron control over his facial expression. But, of course, he was warned when the breakfast hour came and no alarm had been raised. I was afraid of that. How long was he in Naomi's room? Can he possibly know I'm lying? I don't believe so. He was so sure he'd killed her that he didn't check to make sure. It should be easy for him to believe now that she was lying there, keeping quiet, to fool him. It's always so easy to believe the things we're afraid to believe.

Eilers said suddenly, "Bess is feeling a little shaky, Pat. I'm going to take her up to the suite."

Campbell, noting the pasty color of the girl's cheeks, replied with perfunctory concern. "By all means!" He had no need to remind his assistant not to leave Bess alone. He turned his attention back to the table as Eilers and Bess went out of the room toward the stairs.

Francie Dunham said, "What are we going to do? Tomorrow Drake Freedon will be here to read the will. Nomy ought to be here, too."

Campbell said, "Grannat!"

The old butler's thin countenance was gray. "Sir?"

"There's a state policeman in the grove beyond the pump house. Send for him, will you? Tell him I need him in here."

"Yes, sir. Immediately, sir." Grannat went out.

Ranny Overholt said, "A policeman!"

Martin Quest looked at Campbell with annoyance and belligerence on his ugly face. "How long has there been a policeman hanging around these grounds?"

"Since Naomi told me somebody tried to kill her."

"I still don't know whether to believe it or not." Jewell Northrup leaned back in her chair, dropping her hands into her lap. "If you knew Nomy the way we do!"

Quest suddenly looked more tired and long-suffering than angry. "I agree with Jewell, Campbell; I wonder whether to believe it or not. I agree with Ranny, too. Nomy is always playing up the dramatic element in a situation, or creating it if it doesn't already exist. Unless—did you see the wound?"

The detective felt his impatience rising. "I saw the wound, yes," he said tersely. "You can take my word for it: somebody certainly stabbed Naomi last night. The wound was small, a mere speck. The rod used as a weapon couldn't have been more than a quarter inch in diameter."

Francie Dunham said with a gasp, "Oh! The curtain rod!"

"What curtain rod?" Campbell demanded sharply.

"In our bathroom," Sally Mace said, looking at Francie with horror in her eyes, then back at the detective.

"Well, what about the curtain rod?"

Francie said shakily, "It was over the bathroom window. The Koroseal curtain was dusty. Yesterday afternoon I took it down and rinsed the dust off. Then I hung it over a chair to dry before I put it back, and went downstairs and forgot it."

"And she left part of the rod lying on the chair seat," Sally said. "Part of the rod was a hollow brass tube that the other part slipped into. The other part was a solid brass rod about a foot and a half long. That's the part Francie left on the chair; the tube was still hanging on its bracket at one end of the window."

"And that rod was just about a quarter-inch in diameter." Francie's voice had lost some of its shakiness now. "It would have been easy to sharpen it to a point. There are all kinds of tools in the shop out back, and nobody was paying any attention to what anyone else was doing."

"When we came back up to our room," Sally put in, looking up at Campbell, "the rod was gone from the chair. We thought it had rolled off. We looked all over for it and couldn't find it. So we just had Grannat get us another one."

Campbell said, "That could be the weapon used to stab Naomi; it probably was. Anybody else have anything else to add?"

The group at the table was cold sober by this time. No one had any doubt left that for once Naomi Andross had something to be afraid of, with no need for dramatics or histrionics.

Ranny Overholt eyed Campbell sharply. "I take it that you don't want any of us to leave the place for anything, until after the will is read."

"Not only don't leave the place," Campbell answered, "I don't want anyone to leave the house until after I've had a chance to talk to you all privately. Don't, at any time, leave the grounds that immediately surround the house until I give you permission to do so. Our would-be killer may not have struck for the last time, and if he has an opportunity to strike again, he may not miss the next time."

"Oh, dear!" Jewell Northrup bit her lip, and the sound of panic was in her voice. "Who do you—who do you think he'd attack next?"

Campbell rose and stepped back from the table. "Since I'm not certain why he attacked Naomi, how can I answer that? I can only say that any or all of you may be in danger. Stay together, all seven of you; don't go roaming about the house by yourselves. If you'll all do that, he can't harm you."

The butler came in to say that he'd sent for Landis, and that the policeman should be coming in very soon. "The rest of the staff sense that something is wrong, sir. Should I tell them anything?"

The detective said, "They'll have to know sooner or later, Grannat. They'd better know now, they might be of invaluable aid. Tell them there was an attempt to kill Miss Naomi, that no one is to leave the house until further orders, to keep their eyes and ears open and report any irregularity or suspicious circumstance to you."

"Yes, sir. And I will report to you. Are there any other orders now, sir?"

"I'm going out into that little lounge room that opens into the patio, Grannat. I'd like to speak to all the people here in private. You can bring them to me one at a time. I'll be ready for them shortly. When Officer Landis comes in, he'll take over for you, and you may go on and explain to the other members of the staff." He added, as he turned to leave the room, "Come along with me for a moment, will you please, Grannat?"

The butler followed him to the small lounge, which was far enough removed from the breakfast room so that not even the murmur of voices would carry from one room to the other.

Campbell seated himself in the wide lounge chair which stood half-facing the window beside the door opening into the patio. A small end table was near the chair, and he drew the table over in front of him.

Grannat laid a hand on the back of a straight-backed upholstered chair a few feet away. "Would you like this across the table from you, sir?"

"Yes, I would. Thanks very much. I have to tell you something, Grannat. Brace yourself for it. We have a murderer in this house, sitting in there in the breakfast room, passing himself off as an innocent bystander and getting away with it—so far."

The butler's face was still gray, but it did not change expression. "Miss Naomi is really dead, sir?"

"She is. Her body is at the morgue in the coroner's undertaking parlor. I took her there last night. She was still alive when I found her, but she died within a few minutes. I think that the same person who murdered Miss Naomi also killed her father. I don't know what his motive is, unless it's money, and every person in the breakfast room could have that motive. I don't want any of them to know that Miss Naomi is dead, or that I know her father was murdered. The longer I can make the guilty person believe that Miss Naomi is still alive, the more chance I have of tripping him up. Can you trust the other members of the staff to keep this knowledge to themselves?"

"Oh, yes. Without doubt, sir. We've all been with the Andross family for years. There isn't a one of them I wouldn't depend on in any kind of trying circumstance, sir."

"Good! Then put the whole bunch of them wise. You're all my assistants, Grannat. Tell the others that none of the family or guests knows, or will know till I tell them, and see that they don't do any careless inter-staff gossiping where it might be overheard. Tell the gardeners if they see any person trying to leave the grounds to stop him; if such a person should refuse to listen, crown him with a spade or anything that comes handy. Whatever the murderer is trying to achieve, he must get it done before the will is read. The terms of the will change then."

"He hasn't much time, sir."

"No. Today, tonight, and tomorrow till one o'clock."

"You think, sir, if he believes Miss Naomi still alive, he may try to leave here to make another attempt on her life?"

"I hope he does, Grannat. You understand everything, now?"

"Yes, sir. I believe so. Whom shall I send in first, sir?"

"I think I'll talk to Ranny Overholt."

"Yes, sir. I'll tell him." The butler turned and went out of the little lounge, down the hall toward the breakfast room.

12

OVERHOLT CAME IN LOOKING uneasy and anxious, his dark red hair smoothly in place, his hazel-brown eyes inquiring. He slid into the chair across the little table from Campbell and leaned his elbows on the table-top's polished wood. He said immediately, "Jewell disobeyed orders, Campbell, the minute you and Grannat were out of sight."

"What did she do?"

"She went up to Naomi's suite. Jewell's a die-hard. She had to be convinced that Nomy was really gone."

"And did she convince herself?"

"Yes—and the rest of us, too. We all kind of had an idea you might be spoofing us, some kind of put-up job between you and Nomy, and Nomy might be hiding over in the servants' wing. Jewell looked in Nomy's closet. She said Nomy's white hat and shoes and bag were gone, and her blue coat, too."

Campbell said, "And if you look in the garage you'll see that her car is gone. Satisfied?"

Overholt looked a little sheepish. "Sure. That's the outfit she wore out here; it's what she'd wear if she went back to L.A. You know, if the man who attacked Nomy made her believe he was you when he stood right by her and put his arm over her shoulders, that narrows the field."

"Yes? Why?"

"Well, hell! You're no pigmy, you know! Ike's no more than five foot-nine. Mart's only five-four. I'm five foot-eight. Quent Ireland is six-one. The tallest one of the group is Drake Freedon; he's six foot-three, but he isn't here. Nomy's no shrimp herself. Whoever it was had to be taller than she was."

"Or standing on the tread above her to make him appear taller," Campbell said, smiling. "I don't suppose you remember just what you were doing last night?"

"Why shouldn't I? Last week I might not. But my memory isn't that short. Mart and I were playing cribbage for a while, then we tired of that and just sat and talked till we went to bed. We always like to talk."

Campbell sat silent for an instant, thinking back to the previous night, to the hours he had patiently spent patrolling the hall, listening, watching and locking doors. He ran over the details rapidly in swift review.

By nine-thirty the entire party had gone to their rooms. At ten-twenty somebody had lured Naomi out to her death. At eleven-twenty-five he had rapped at Naomi's door and heard what he thought was her voice answering. At twelve-ten, or a few seconds before, he had found Naomi dying and carried her to his and Eilers' suite. Somewhere along that corridor of time there had been some split-second thinking and acting.

He was not dealing with a murderer who would give himself away easily or carelessly.

The detective looked steadily at Overholt across the little table, remembering what Ranny had just said about his memory not being short, about liking to talk to Mart Quest. It wouldn't seem that anyone could have slipped out of any of those rooms, could have engaged in any murderous activities, in between all those carefully checked intervals. But somebody had.

Campbell said, "How long were you playing crib?"

"Oh, I don't know. You don't ordinarily notice things like that, you know. Till we were tired of it. Must have been somewhere around eleven when we quit, I guess."

A few minutes before eleven. Yes. That checked. Campbell had locked their door at eleven. "I suppose you could get in and out of the window some way, if you'd wanted to?"

"Take a look out that window and you'll change your mind. Not a toe-hold or a hand-hold anywhere."

"How'd you happen to notice that, Ranny?"

"I don't know. I just did notice it. You'd have to use a ladder, unless you wanted to chance breaking a leg. See here, Campbell; if you've got any ideas about my slipping out of my room and sticking a curtain rod in Naomi, you can discard them right now. Not that I haven't felt sometimes that she had something of the kind coming to her. She can be an awful heel when she wants to. I was right there in the suite, playing cribbage and yarning. Ask Mart if you don't believe me."

Campbell said, "Don't get your dander up. I have to ask these questions."

Overholt ran a hand over his dark red hair, and smiled a little sheepishly. "Excuse it, please. I didn't mean to sound testy. Go on and ask. I'll be as glad as any of the others to help in any way I can."

"Then see if you can think of anything that would help me get a clue to Naomi's assailant."

Overholt frowned and shook his head. "Sorry, but I don't know a thing to tell. It's too bad Naomi couldn't get a good look at him."

"I agree with you. It's a pretty easy thing, though, to slip up on an unsuspecting person in the dark—especially when the person is morally sure there is nothing to fear at the moment."

Overholt nodded, sobered completely. "Yeah. That's right. I shouldn't have popped off the way I did about her. But she's always dramatizing and imagining. I thought this was another of those times. I didn't realize her life had really been in danger."

"You know it now."

"Yeah. It's rather unnerving. When's Naomi coming back? She'll be here in time to hear the will read, won't she?"

"She didn't say anything about coming back. I guess that's all I want of you right now, Ranny. Tell Mrs. Northrup to come in, will you?"

"Yes. Of course." Overholt still looked pale and upset. He went out of the lounge in a hurry, both hands plunged into his pockets.

Jewell Northrup came in looking a great deal more composed than she had been when Campbell last saw her in the breakfast room. She took the chair facing him and asked quietly, "What can I tell you, Mr. Campbell?"

"You were pretty close to Naomi ever since her childhood, I'd guess, weren't you? Nothing's ever changed that, you're still as close to her now that she's grown?"

"Yes. I've been like a second mother to her in many ways. She has always confided in me a lot."

"That's what I was hoping. Has she ever admitted to you that she thought her father was murdered?"

Jewell's voice caught and lowered. "Yes. She hasn't admitted it to anyone else. I haven't even told Ike."

"Did she say whether she had any idea who the murderer might be?"

"No, she didn't have any idea. That was what frightened her." Jewell Northrup gave him a long, steady stare. "See here, Mr. Campbell; Naomi's dead, isn't she? You're just trying to keep us from finding it out."

Campbell said, "You saw that her clothes were gone, didn't you?"

"Yes. Yes, that's right. I suppose you're being honest with us. It's just like Nomy to go rushing off that way; especially in view of her secret conviction that Wark was murdered, and after someone tried to kill her, too. I can't imagine anyone wanting to harm that child, Mr. Campbell. I've always loved her like my own. She's *been* like my own since her mother died. My only little girl died in her infancy; she was just a month older than Naomi. Naomi has taken her place for Ike and me, in our lives and in our hearts. Naomi has her faults, as who hasn't, but it's a pretty pale affection that balks at a few little human faults. I wish you'd tell me, please; was she really hurt very much? I can't bear to think of her being sick or hurt and me not with her to take care of her."

"I'm not going to make things any harder for you, Mrs. Northrup," the detective said gently. "It isn't fair. But I must ask you not to repeat it to anyone, not even to Mr. Northrup. Naomi is at peace, nothing can ever hurt her again."

Jewell's face quivered, and her eyes filled. "Oh! Oh, God. She's dead. He did kill her!"

"Yes. She lived only a few moments after I found her. She couldn't tell me anything to help identify him."

Jewell forced her face into composure and blinked the tears from her eyes. "Where is she? I want to see her."

"She's at an undertaking parlor. You can't see her, not yet. You have to help me deceive the others into thinking she's still alive. You have to help me find the person who killed her, and Wark."

The woman sat erect, her plump hands gripped at the waist below her stout breasts. "Yes. I'll be all right. You needn't worry about my giving anything away. I'll do anything—*anything,* to help. The poor child! Think of it! Somebody stabbing her with a—what did you say it was? Oh, that's right. You weren't sure. Do you think it could possibly be that curtain rod Francie was talking about? That seems awfully far-fetched."

"Perhaps. But it's quite possible. A brass rod of that type would be rigid and strong. It would be a perfect weapon for the purpose, and I understand there's a shop out back fitted with all sorts of tools. Anyone would have had plenty of opportunity to sharpen it. Would you take on a job for me, Mrs. Northrup? Would you go on an unobtrusive hunt for that rod? You might enlist the help of the servants. They know Naomi is dead."

"Will I? I'll start right now!" Jewell got to her feet, one plump hand braced against the table top. "You don't want me for anything more, do you?"

"I'd like to know just one thing, if you don't mind telling me. What were you and Ike quarreling about last night?"

Jewell gave a short, disgusted laugh. "That man! He wanted me to go and get you right then, so he could tell you what he knew about Wark arguing with somebody by the pool the night he was killed. He doesn't believe Wark fell in, either. He thinks somebody pushed him. I wouldn't go bothering you at that time of night, he said he'd go after you himself, I said he wouldn't—and we just went on from there. You know how it is once you get started fussing. I finally shut him up; I said he could tell you in the morning."

Campbell said, "He can tell me now. Send him in, will you?"

"Yes, I will. Right away. And I won't tell him about Nomy. Ike never can keep his mouth shut. He'd tell everybody in the house. He'd be so furious he'd ruin every plan you might have for trapping the murderer. Oh, I know him, Mr. Campbell. He's a good man, and he loved Nomy. But he's no man to keep a secret. Where do you think I should start looking for that rod?"

"God knows, Mrs. Northrup. Your guess is as good as mine. Mainly, I thought you'd be better off with something to do."

"And that's the truth!" Her plump chin quivered again, and she dashed one hand across her eyes to wipe away threatening tears. "If I had just to sit around and think of that poor child, I'd go crazy. I'll send Ike right in to you."

As she went out of the room Grannat stepped to the door to speak to the detective. "Officer Landis has just come in, sir. He'd like to speak to you. He's out back waiting."

Campbell rose quickly. "I'll go right out. Hold Ike Northrup up till I get back, Grannat."

"Yes, sir."

Landis was pacing impatiently just outside the service porch, an uneasy frown on his face. The frown did not clear as the big detective emerged from the house and approached rapidly. Landis stopped short, and said in an undertone, "Good thing you sent for me. I was about to take the bull by the horns and come to the house after you."

"What's happened?"

"I saw somebody monkeying around among the trees over

yonder. I hiked over, but whoever it was had gone. You know that light you saw as we were coming into the canyon. I wondered if it was somebody who oughtn't to be there with a light, and if the person in the trees was the same one who'd been making the light."

"Did you take time to investigate?"

"In the trees just now? No, only to make sure that somebody'd been there all right. There was a smashed place as if someone had been lying there, maybe all night."

Campbell said, "Come on. Show me."

Landis led the way back from the house to the smashed place under the trees. Campbell walked about, looking for some small thing that might have been left by the prowler. There was no doubt that Landis had judged correctly. Someone must have been lying there for rather a long while, several hours at least, to make such an impression on the wild grass and small plants.

He found several cigarette stubs poked into a hollow under a small shrub with a few burned paper match ends. He picked up the longest of the stubs, raised himself erect and held it up for Landis to see. The tip of the stub was smudged with lipstick.

Campbell said, "Our prowler was a lady, George."

"Huh? Well, I'll be damned! Now, why the hell would any woman be pulling a stunt like that?"

Campbell dropped the cigarette stub into his pocket. "Waiting for a chance to get into the house, George. She wasn't just spying; I'd bet on it."

"What makes you think that?"

"Because I think I know who she was. And I think you could call her Miss Taylor and she'd answer to the name."

Landis said, "Oh. You want me to range around and pick her up?"

Campbell shook his head. "No. She'll show up when she gets ready. She isn't going to bother anybody. Not now, at any rate. We might as well go along back to the house."

The state policeman followed the detective out of the trees, and went with him down the path, across the patio and through the side door into the lounge.

"You making any headway with these people yet, Pat?"

"It's too early to tell. But gradually a few things are showing up. I don't want any of them to learn that Naomi's dead yet, except the servants and Mrs. Northrup. They're all beyond suspicion. I've told the others she was attacked, frightened out, and went back to L.A. It looks now as if the weapon used were a sharpened brass curtain rod. Ride herd on them while I put them through the mill, will you? Keep them right there in the breakfast room, all but Mrs. Northrup."

"She's a relative, or something?"

"Right. She was Naomi's mother's sister and very fond of the girl; second-mother sort of set-up. If she wants to go roaming around, let her. That's all, George."

Landis nodded acquiescence, and started off toward the breakfast room.

Campbell rang for the butler, and Grannat came in from the back of the house. Campbell said, "You can go talk with the rest of the staff, now, Grannat."

"Yes, sir. Thanks very much. I'll tell them right away what's happened, and what they're to do."

Campbell went over to the little table and sat down again, one hand in his pocket. His fingers touched the cigarette stub smudged with lipstick. He thought the girl hadn't wasted much time following Bess to the Canyon House. She wouldn't have had any trouble finding the place. She could take a bus to Logus. Almost anyone in the town could tell her where to find Flour Gold Canyon.

Campbell looked up as Ike Northrup came into the little lounge, to pause beside the table.

Ike said, "Jewell told me you wanted to see me, Pat. Grannat said you'd gone out with the policeman. I was waiting for you to come back."

Campbell said, "That's right, Ike."

"She was kind of mad. You pink her on a sore spot?"

Campbell said, "I asked her what you and she were jawing about last night."

"Oh." Northrup sobered, his slow smile of greeting fading at Campbell's words. "We were talking about Wark. I don't like to see such things covered up. Plain criminal, that's what it is. Wark Andross diving into seven inches of water? Like hell he did. He was pushed, that's what. And Mart Quest did it. Mart, Ranny and Quent were all in there by the pool arguing with him for almost an hour before Thibault found him."

"How do you know that?"

"Nomy and I were out getting a basketful of night-blooming cereus, that's how I know. You ever seen a *hylocereus ocamponis* bloom?"

"No. Afraid I haven't."

"It's something to see. Ever notice that tall glass house on the second terrace, east side of the hill?"

Campbell nodded. "Yes. I've noticed it."

"That's where the *hylocereus* is. Ratty looking plant, a lot of frosty-pale arms crawling up to the roof like snakes. But the blossoms! Anywhere from twenty to thirty long narrow petals, sort of yellowish in the middle and rimmed with red. They spread out in a sort of scanty fringe behind the real flower. It's white. Same number of petals, wide and overlapping, look like white silk. A thick spread of yellow stamens in the middle. The blooms measure from ten to twelve inches across."

"And they bloom only at night?"

"That's right. If you pick 'em before dark they never open quite so wide. Naomi was crazy about 'em. We'd always take a flashlight and go down to the glass house and get them after they'd open up. Then she'd put 'em in a bowl and take 'em up to her room."

"And that's what you were doing that night?"

"That's right. We took the basket and went along, and as we passed the big pool we heard Wark and Quent and Ranny and Mart all talking. Mart was talking pretty loud. Nomy said, 'What the hell's going on in there?' But we didn't take it too seriously. Somebody was always ragging about something in that house. By the time we got to the glass house, and I had crawled around with a step ladder and clipped off the blossoms, it had taken us forty-five minutes."

"And you came back by the pool?"

"We did, purposely. We wanted to see whether the argument was still going on. It was. But Quent and Ranny had gone; all the jawing was between Wark and Mart now. They both sounded mad. Nomy and I didn't like it, but we didn't butt in. Nomy took the basket and went on to the house. I ran into Quent beyond the cypress windbreak, and he was a little bothered about the fuss; we could hear Mart and Wark still arguing. Then Quent and I went on to the house. I didn't see Martin again that night. And the next thing I knew about Wark he was dead."

"What were Wark and Martin Quest arguing about?"

"About Wark's will. I hate to say anything to get the boy into trouble, but if he killed Wark I want to see him get what's coming to him."

"In what way was the will concerned?"

"Mart was trying to persuade Wark to change it. We heard Wark say, 'I won't change that will and you might as well shut up about it.' Mart said, 'I won't shut up; I'll keep on raising hell till you do change it. I don't like it and I won't have it.' Then Quent and I were too far past to hear anything further."

"That was all you heard?"

"Yes. Except for the sound of their voices. We weren't trying to listen in, you know."

"Did you know Anne Elizabeth?" Campbell asked. He wondered if he would hit a mark this time. One isn't likely to notice a change of that kind unless the name is pretty familiar. He'd tried it out on Eilers; he'd called her Anne Elizabeth two or three times and Eilers hadn't noticed it, even after having looked up the vital statistics. It didn't work now.

Ike Northrup said, "Anne Elizabeth who?"

"It doesn't matter," Campbell said. "I was merely wondering if you knew her."

"Never heard of her."

"You didn't happen to be in the vicinity of the tool shop at any time yesterday afternoon and hear any of the power tools going?"

"No. I wasn't out of the house yesterday afternoon. I usually take a nap after lunch."

"What do you know about Wark's will?"

"Not a damn thing. He said he was going to leave a bit to Jewell and me, and we thought it was handsome of him, but we certainly didn't go around building castles on the idea and we never even hinted that he should name the amount of the bequest."

"You've no idea what it may be yourself?"

"Oh, I wouldn't be surprised if he left us ten or fifteen grand. Wark was a generous man. Jewell doesn't think it would be over five. What of it? Whatever he left us will be appreciated, even if it should be no more than a hundred-dollar bill. We didn't like Wark for his money. We liked him because he was Wark."

The detective smiled. "Most people did. Yet, somebody killed him for that money, Ike."

"I know. It's hard to grasp. Impossible to understand. A man like Wark. Any sonofagun as greedy as that—the gas chamber's too easy. I'd like to stand and watch him fry in the hot seat."

Campbell said pleasantly, "So would I. I can't think of anything further I want to ask you now, Ike. Tell Officer Landis to send Quentin Ireland in, will you?"

Northrup went out, walking slowly, his face somber. Once he looked back at Campbell, as if he had thought of something, but he didn't speak. He only shook his head and went on.

13

IRELAND'S TALL SPARE FIGURE came into the lounge silently as a shadow. His dark slightly wolfish face was openly concerned, his manner perturbed. He said quietly, "I passed Ike in the doorway. He said for me to tell you he has an uncomfortable feeling that Naomi is dead, that maybe she never reached Beverly Hills, that if she did get there she died of her wound before she could get help. He thought a lot of her, you know. He wanted me to ask whether you'd phoned in to check and see if she's all right. But I guess you haven't been out of the house since she left, have you? Wark wanted to be completely isolated when he came out here; he never would have a phone. You'd have to go to Logus to phone."

Campbell gestured toward the chair across the table. "Sit down, Ireland, and take it easy. No, I haven't been out of the house since Naomi left. You mean Quest had to go to Logus when he telephoned to Drake Freedon Sunday, then? When he called him for Nomy?"

"Yes. He was gone for over an hour. What do you think about it, Campbell? You think maybe she could be lying dead somewhere, and none of us the wiser? I can't help worrying about that. That was one thing about her—she always minimized any physical pain or hurt. She could be half dying, and she'd say it was only a scratch. You don't think she could have died on the way to Beverly Hills, or after she got there?"

"I can say no to that very positively, so let's change the subject. You were reading last night before you went to bed, weren't you? I heard you turning pages—I was patrolling the hall."

"Oh? Yes, I was reading some new magazines I brought out with me. I thought I heard someone walking in the hall a time or two. Too bad you didn't connect with the rat who tried to do Naomi in. She was a good kid, basically, you know. Too damned good for Drake Freedon. He's a stuffed shirt if ever I saw one."

Campbell said, "By the way, Ireland—when you were out for a hike yesterday, which way did you come in? After you neared the buildings, I mean."

"I came in via the graveled path and the flagstone walk, past the pump house. Look, Campbell, you don't take any stock in that curtain rod business, do you? Kind of wild, isn't it?"

"Wild? No. Not if you knew some of the murder weapons that have been used. Our murderer wouldn't have used a gun even if he could have got hold of one. He wanted this to be a quiet job. He might not have had anything in his possession to answer the purpose. He couldn't get a knife from the kitchen without being seen by Sophronia or one of the footmen or the maids, or Grannat. To ask for it would have been foolish, and he's not a fool. He probably started prowling about the rooms upstairs to see what he could find, and went into the girls' room hoping to pick up a nail file, a pair of scissors, maybe a knitting needle, the sort of things girls can be expected to carry. He saw the rod lying on the chair, and thought of the tools in the shop. He took it and got out of there."

A faint grin wrinkled Ireland's thin face. "You could think up a pretty good homicide yourself, couldn't you?"

"I've committed murder a hundred times, in my mind, trying to move one step ahead of the man I was after. You weren't near enough to the house on your stroll to notice anyone going to or coming from the tool shop, were you?"

"No, and I wouldn't have thought anything of it if I had. Everybody was all over the place. Except Ike Northrup. He was lying down taking a snooze. Always does in the afternoon. If you're through with me, do you mind if I run into Logus and call Nomy? Just to set my mind at rest about her?"

Campbell said, "I'm through with you. And I do mind your going into Logus. When I said I wanted everybody to stay in the house till further orders, I meant everybody."

Ireland rose from the impromptu examination chair. "All right. I'll stay put. Want me to send in anybody? Mart, or somebody?"

"I don't want to see Mart yet. I would like to talk to Francie Dunham and Sally Mace. They can come in together." He thought, watching Ireland amble loosely out of the room, that the girls were a pair of chatterboxes when they were in each other's company; they seemed to affect each other that way. They'd be more likely to let something slip when they both had their tongues going. Francie in particular was inclined to be serious and quiet without Sally to prompt her, he'd noticed.

He rose and fetched another chair. He had barely settled again in his own seat when the girls came in, arm in arm. He waved them to the two chairs, side by side, smiling at them. Youth, he thought. How we miss that spontaneous feeling of being alive and feeling as if we'd live forever, once our own youth's gone and we view it in somebody else! The girls sat down, holding hands as if to give each other moral support and encouragement.

Francie said immediately, "I know. Naomi's dead. You're going to tell us Nomy's dead."

"I'm going to tell you nothing of the kind. I'm only going to ask you a few questions. I know pretty well what you were doing last night from about nine-thirty on; everybody in the house could have heard you giggling and snickering, I imagine. And I could hear Sally reading, caught some of the words now and then. I was on the verge of asking you to pipe down, when you finally hit the hay. What I want to know about is this morning. Were you girls out of your room at any time before you came down to breakfast long enough for somebody to go into your quarters without being seen by either of you?"

Sally answered promptly. "No. But somebody was in our room when we were there."

"Oh, yes? Who?"

"Ranny and Mart." Sally slid a sidelong glance at Francie. "Francie and Mart are engaged, you know."

"So I'd heard."

"Well, Ranny and Mart stopped to pick us up on their way down to breakfast. But we weren't ready. Francie still had her hair in curlers."

Francie flashed Campbell a humorous glance. "And Sally had cold cream all over her face. She uses it for a powder base."

"So Ranny and Mart decided not to wait?" the detective asked.

"Well, no. At first they thought they would wait," Francie said. "I got busy taking down my hair, and Sally started wiping off the cold cream."

"What did Mart and Ranny do?"

"Mart sat down and kidded Francie," Sally said.

Francie said, "And Ranny wanted to go to our bathroom."

"He could have gone to the bathroom in his own suite before he started down to breakfast. Why didn't he?"

"Because the flush bowl in their bathroom was all clogged up," Sally said.

"Then after he came out, he got tired of waiting for us to doll up. He said he was too hungry to appreciate the applied art of cosmetics, and besides he always did hate to see a girl make up her face. So he and Mart went on. We told them we'd get to the table almost as soon as they did." Francie smiled at Sally. "We weren't far behind them, either."

Campbell said, "I don't suppose either of you ever heard of Anne Elizabeth, did you?"

Francie cocked her head on one side doubtfully. "I don't think so. Did we, Sally?"

"Not that I can remember. Is she somebody important?"

"Not so far as you two are concerned. What time was it yesterday afternoon when you left that rod on the chair?"

"Oh, I don't know. Right after noon somewhere," Francie said. "It must have been a couple of hours later when we went back and found it gone and asked Grannat to get another one."

"You wouldn't know who might have been upstairs at any time in your absence from your room?"

Sally said, "The only one who was upstairs that we knew of was Mr. Northrup. Mrs. Northrup tried to get him to lie down in the swing, but he said who wanted to break his ribs on hard board slats when there was a good soft bed to lie on."

"We were out in the yard ourselves," Francie said. "Anybody could have gone upstairs a dozen times and we wouldn't have noticed it."

Campbell said, "Well, I believe that's all. Tell Mart I'd like to speak to him, will you? I'll let you all scatter out of the breakfast room pretty soon, now."

The girls went out, and the detective made a mental note of the fact that neither one had commented on the likelihood of the rod being made into a weapon. It seemed to have slipped their minds entirely that such an idea had been discussed before in the breakfast room.

He was still thinking about it, wondering whether it could have any possible significance, when Quest came down the hall with his oddly light and springing step. Campbell thought again of an athlete in miniature, as he watched the small perfectly proportioned figure near the table and pause by the chair where Sally had been sitting.

Quest said, "I hope you've rounded up some worthwhile information. What can I do for you, Pat?" He slid gracefully into the chair and surveyed Campbell with polite inquiry.

The detective looked curiously into the ugly face crowned by the large bald head. "I hope you can do a lot for me, Mart. And I hope you won't do any hedging."

"I don't know why I should do any hedging," Quest said, "I couldn't be of much help that way. I'll give you a straight answer to any question you ask."

"Very well, then. You won't deny you were talking to Wark the night he died, you and Ranny and Ireland. And you were there alone talking to Wark after Ranny and Quent Ireland left."

"That's so; I certainly was."

"Well, there's one thing I particularly want to know, Mart. Didn't Wark, or any of you, notice that the pool was low?"

Quest stared a little. "Notice it? Of course we noticed it! If we hadn't, Wark would have called our attention to it. He was mad and disappointed; he'd come out to swim, there was a swell moon, and the damned pool was empty, save for a few inches on the bottom."

"He was angry with Ransome?"

"He sure was! He said he'd sent him orders to clean the pool, Saturday evening, by Thibault; Ransome had had plenty of time to get it done, and here was the pool still draining."

"None of you shut the sluice gate, then?"

"Why, no. Why would we shut it? We supposed Ransome was draining it so he could clean it the next day."

"How'd you all happen to be there with Wark?"

"He invited us to have a swim with him. We didn't care about a swim, but we went along for company. When we found the pool empty, we sat down on the tile and talked. Ranny and Quent left, Wark and I got into a little harangue, and finally I got mad and went out and slammed the gate, leaving him in there by himself."

"So he was alive the last time you saw him? I hope you'll tell me the truth now, Mart."

Mart Quest said, "You can depend on that."

"Then, do you mind telling me what you and Wark were quarreling about that evening a little while before he was killed?"

"Killed!" Quest echoed. "So you didn't believe it was an accident. Nomy and I cooked that story up before Wheeler came, Pat. We knew from scratch that somebody had done Wark in. But I couldn't persuade Nomy to let me call the police. She was so damned scared that she was on the verge of hysterics. Wark always hated fuss and publicity so badly, she wanted to keep it quiet until after the will was read. Then she was going to call in a detective on the quiet, and set him to work on turning up the killer."

Campbell said, "I see. She had reason to believe her own life would be in great danger until the will was read?"

"She certainly did! You know the terms of the will?"

"Most of them, I believe. Freedon gave me an outline."

"I hate physical labor," Quest said, a humorous smile baring his big crooked teeth. "I hate the idea of being a man with a job, sunk in a rut. Wark and I got along. I always tried to earn my board by being a kind of personal handy man and errand boy for him. I liked doing it and I saved him a lot of headaches that way. Wark was grateful and made sure I could continue to live decently after he was gone. He willed me a million bucks. Any man who can't be happy on a million iron men ought to have his head examined."

"So that wasn't the point of the altercation?"

"No. If he'd stopped there, it would have been all right. Did you know he'd been married before? Before he married Sharon?"

Campbell said, "You're thinking of Anne Elizabeth?" The trick paid out then, for what it was worth, if anything. The detective thought a man had to try all sorts of tricks to bring concealed bits into the open. Sometimes they were the right bits.

Quest said, "You have the names transposed. Her name was Elizabeth Anne. Wark evidently spoke of her to you. So let's stop this silly question-and-answer game and get down to cases. I remember Elizabeth Anne fairly well. I was fourteen years old when she and Mary left Seattle. That pseudo-secretary of yours is practically a reincarnation of Elizabeth Anne as far as size and coloring are concerned. She even looks a little like Wark when she smiles. She's Mary Elizabeth Andross, and

Holloway was her mother's maiden name. So don't let's horse around with that kind of crap. I even remember Mary herself. But a kid changes a lot in twenty years."

Campbell said, "All right. We'll take it straight from the shoulder then, Mart. What was the proviso you wanted Wark to change?"

"I didn't want him to change it. I wanted him to omit it entirely. It was the will I wanted changed, by that omission. It was a paragraph in which he stated that if either of the girls should die before the will was read, the other girl was to get her share. If both should be deceased when the will was read, the entire sum was to go to me. Worst damned foolishness I ever heard of."

"You mean you wouldn't want to inherit seven millions at that possible price?"

"You're damned tooting I mean it. I'd like to roll in seven million dollars as well as any man—but not if two girls had to die to pass it on to me. Look what kind of spot that put me in!"

"Well? What kind of spot did it put you in?"

Quest glared. "You know what I mean! A man would have to be pretty strong-willed not to play with the idea. I'm not that strong-willed."

"You tell Wark that?"

"Certainly I told him. That was what started the row. The further condition of the paragraph is that if either girl dies intestate after the will is read, her share goes to an organization for the blind."

"Yes, I know," Campbell said. "That's about what Freedon said that day when he was talking to me. Did Wark ever explain to you his reason for such a paragraph?"

"Oh, yes. If either girl should die before the will was read, the money would never really have been hers, you see. They were his daughters. He wanted them to have all of it; either of them, or both of them, whichever should be living. After the girls came into the money, he wanted them to have the privilege of making their own wills and naming their own legatees. Hence the intestate clause."

"I see. It would be reasonable from Wark's point of view."

"But it's a murder trap!" Quest said excitedly. "It's a God damned murder trap! If I were the kind of bird who wouldn't turn a hair at cinching a big inheritance by killing off the two girls, see what an incentive it would dangle before my eyes."

Campbell said, "Yours or any other man's, Mart. You're quite right, it would be a strong-willed man who wouldn't at least play with the idea if he brooded over it long enough."

"You know it!"

"And you told Wark all this?"

"In almost the same words I've just expressed to you."

"But see here, Mart—since you're not the sort of man to kill off two girls to get the tempting seven millions, why did you raise cain with Wark about it? Because you were afraid of yourself?"

Quest's excitement subsided. "Because," he said slowly, "because there's another paragraph. Freedon evidently didn't mention that one to you. Maybe he doesn't consider it so important. I wanted Wark to cut that out of the will, too."

"And it provided what?"

"That in the event the two girls and I should all be dead when the will was read, the seven million was to be equally divided among Jewell Northrup, Ike Northrup, and Francie Dunham, who is in a fashion distantly related. If the whole damned shooting match should be deceased at the time of the reading, the entire seven million would go to the organization for the blind. Wark wanted his money to stay in the family if possible, and the will admonishes all of us to do as much good as we can with our inheritance instead of spending it all for our own personal pleasures. Wark was nothing if not thorough! That proviso naming the organization for the blind, was just a sort of last ditch arrangement, for which he never expected there to be any need, but just in case—he wanted to order the ultimate disposition of his fortune instead of letting the state do it."

"It's a sweet set-up for anybody who's money-hungry, isn't it?"

"That's what I tried to tell Wark. I tried to persuade him to make it all out in straight bequests and let it go at that. If anybody was dead and couldn't inherit, the state would spread it around among the living relatives anyhow. He didn't want that, and he wouldn't have it. I couldn't budge him. That will still stands."

"Do the Northrups and Francie know about this?"

"I don't think so. That is, I didn't think so, till you sprung your bomb on us at the breakfast table this morning. Now, I'm not so sure. Somebody knows too damned much. Wark was killed, wasn't he? Nomy was murdered, wasn't she? And let's not horse around about that, either. I know she's dead, and you know she's dead. Let the others think she's still alive if it will help to flush the guilty man out from cover. But you and I don't have to play kids' games. I knew Nomy. If she'd been hurt in an attack such as you described, the last thing she'd have done would have been to turn tail and run to get out of harm's way. She'd have had the whole house kicked out of bed and hauled over the coals. She'd have had half the police in California here before daylight. She'd have made so damned much hullabaloo that six murderers could have slipped through the edges and got away scot free. But—take it lying down and skip for L.A.? Uh-uh! Not Nomy. And you didn't make up that attack story just to hear your ears rattle. Ergo— Nomy was attacked, all right, and she was killed. And you're trying to smoke out a killer by keeping a tight mouth on what happened. Okay, I'm with you. But don't feed me any pap."

Campbell laughed a little, in spite of himself. "You're a sort of firebrand, aren't you, Mart?"

"I'd hate to be wishy-washy. I'm usually slow to suspect or accuse; I'm not accusing Jewell or Ike now, and God knows I couldn't suspect Francie of the sort of money-lust that leads to murder. But there you are. Wark and Nomy. Mary Elizabeth and I will be next on the list. In that order. I know you're keeping a tight guard over Mary."

Campbell put in, "She's called Bess, now."

"Bess or no Bess, she'll always be Mary to me. She was always Mary to Wark. I knew from the way you've been guarding her that you expected trouble. I suppose Eilers is armed?" Quest said.

"He is, naturally. And so am I—naturally. You know, Mart, what you say about Naomi raising hell isn't consistent with her avoiding publicity because Wark hated it so much."

"Oh, yes it is. She wouldn't have blown up a whisper concerning Wark himself. But let somebody try to fit her for a coffin and she'd turn hell upside down! That's a horse of a different color."

"I guess it is. Just for the record, how did you and Ranny spend the evening last night?"

"Didn't he tell you? Played crib till somewhere around eleven, chewed the fat for a while and went to bed."

"And neither one of you left the room at any time all evening?"

"Ranny did, once. Didn't he tell you?"

"No. Neither did he say in so many words that he hadn't left the room, but he inferred it. I suggested he might have gone in or out the window, and he said you'd need a ladder unless you wanted to risk breaking a leg. He said if I had any ideas about him slipping out of his room and sticking a curtain rod in Naomi, I could discard them. I didn't ask him in so many words whether or not he'd left the room, either. I thought I'd ask you."

Quest said impatiently, "The damn fool kid! I told him to tell you he'd been out."

"When? When did you tell him?"

"When you were in here talking to Grannat, just before you sent for Ranny. He's only a crazy kid, and he was scared pink it would look bad for him if you knew he'd been out. Would you mind telling me when Naomi was killed?"

"I found her a little after midnight. Still alive, but she only lived a few minutes. I'll save you asking if she had any idea who killed her. She didn't."

"Ranny had all his worry for nothing, then, the poor sap. We thought we'd like to have a few drinks to help the crib game along, so he went downstairs and brought up a bottle of bourbon. He wasn't gone fifteen minutes, and I heard the clock strike ten-thirty just before he came in. So you know what time he was out of the suite. He didn't leave the room again all evening, and I didn't go out at all."

Campbell said, "Hmmm. I was trying to think where I was right about that time."

"You were in your room. I knew who Mary was the minute I laid eyes on her, of course. I knew you'd be keeping an eye on her. I asked Ranny if you were on watch in the hall. He said no, you were in the suite. He heard you talking to Eilers as he passed the door. Anything more I can tell you?"

"No— Not now, Mart. Unless—does Ranny know anything about Bess, or Mary, as you call her?"

"Not to my knowledge. And if he did, he'd have spoken of it. He tells me everything. My mother brought us both up, you know, after Ranny's folks died. He's always been like my own kid brother; the only brother I've ever had."

"Well, don't tell him about Nomy—or anybody else. Keep it dark until I break the news myself."

"To quote you, naturally." Quest rose, as if his muscles were springs. "You may rest easy. I can keep my lip buttoned. Anything you want me to do?"

"Not at the present. Except to watch out, Mart, and don't get off in any corners by yourself. You might send Grannat in as you go out."

14

THE BUTLER SAID, "MR. QUEST said you wanted me, sir."

Campbell shoved his chair back from the little table and stood up. "Yes. When you got that new curtain rod for Miss Dunham, where did you have to go for it?"

"In the storage closet off the back hall, sir."

"If you'd go there now and count the rods, could you be certain whether that one had been put back?"

"I'm afraid not, sir. There are at least two dozen of them, of all sizes. I didn't pay any attention. I simply fetched the rod and fixed the curtain for Miss Dunham. But it could scarcely be put back when it's still in the curtain, sir, could it?"

"I was just thinking of different angles, Grannat. I suppose the rest of the staff is on the alert?"

"Yes, sir! Indeed they are, sir! You have a corps of able and willing helpers, and they're behaving very sensibly, too."

"That's good. And that's all for the present, Grannat. I've a few little chores to take care of. I'll see you around, later."

Grannat took himself off, and Campbell went to the door of the breakfast room, to speak to Landis. The entire company was still at the table, including Jewell Northrup. The detective said to the state policeman, making no effort to lower his voice, "Keep the folks here for just a few moments longer, George. Then we'll get together."

He went on down the wide hall to the stairway and up to

the second floor. He went into the room occupied by the two girls. The maids had done up the beds and the room was neat and orderly. The detective went on into the bathroom, and up to the small window over which the plastic curtain hung. He stood for a moment looking at it, and he thought, Do I hit the jackpot or draw a blank? If I were in his shoes, that's what I'd do with it. It's about the last place on earth anyone would look for it.

He reached up and removed the right-hand end of the curtain from its bracket. The rod was one of the adjustable type, made to fit a window anywhere from two and a half to four feet wide. The solid rod which slid into the hollow tube sheath could be pushed into the tube its entire length, as it must be for this small window, or let out until there was barely enough of the rod in the sheath to hold rod and tube together. Both rod and tube were tightly fastened at the outer end to a solid brass ornament, molded into the shape of a strawberry with two leaves, roughly about the size of a small egg.

Campbell pushed the curtain back till nearly the entire tube was bared, then he gripped the brass strawberry and began to pull on the rod. The rod fitted snugly into the tube, but it yielded to force easily. Inch by inch it emerged (Sally had said it was about a foot and a half long—it *would be* a foot and a half long were it the rod Grannat had put there); it cleared the tube three inches, four, six, eight—then it fell out into the detective's hand. Rod and strawberry ornament together now were no more than nine and a half inches long.

Campbell gripped the strawberry tightly, a wicked and stout handle. He stared down at the rod, his mouth grim. It had been cut off neatly, the end of it ground to a needle point. It had been washed and wiped carefully, but at the base of the strawberry in the sharp indentation where it joined the rod there was a rusty brown stain which was completely hidden when rod and tube were together. He knew he held in his hand the weapon that had killed Naomi Andross.

The killer had come into this bathroom with the weapon hidden on his person. He had removed from the tube the rod Grannat had placed there. Campbell glanced around the small tiled room. Where had the killer put the rod Grannat had brought up for the girls? There was no place here where it could have been hidden. What had he done with the section of rod he had cut off when he made the weapon?

The detective thumped the end of the sheath against his palm. The other ten and a half inches of the weapon rod slid out into his hand. Campbell put it back into the tube. He pushed the weapon into the tube after the severed piece of rod, set the rod back on its bracket and rearranged the plastic curtain. He shoved up the window and craned his neck, to peer down at the roof below the window. He could see no sign of the missing rod, the one Grannat had furnished. He closed the window, went out of the bathroom, into the hall and down to his own suite.

Bess roused in her chair with a half gasp as he came in. "Mr. Campbell! I want to go home. I'm afraid of this place."

Eilers glanced at him over Bess' head. Campbell said, "I'm afraid you'll have to stay here till the will is read. Eilers and I won't let anything happen to you. You have nothing to be afraid of, if you stay close to Rick and obey orders, Bess."

"I don't want to stay!" She shuddered, and her genuine fright was apparent. "I don't care about the money any more. I just want to go home."

Campbell said, "Sorry, Bess. Can't be done. Take it easy and trust me and Rick. I have to go along. Everything's under control at the moment, Rick. We'll try to keep it that way."

Eilers didn't ask whether there was anything new. He knew from the detective's face that there was, and he knew, too, he would hear it when he and Campbell had a moment alone together.

The detective went back downstairs, released the group from the breakfast room, and sat down to confer with Landis.

The day passed quickly and without event, but there was hard strain in the air, the strain of waiting, of people keeping together because they were afraid to be apart. The entire group stayed in the living room most of the time. They went in to dinner in a close formation, they came back the same way. If one of the girls had to leave the room, the other girl and Jewell Northrup went with her, and their absence was of short duration. The conduct of the men followed the same pattern.

Eilers and Bess stayed downstairs most of the day, largely because Bess wanted plenty of company around her. She had taken something of a fancy to Ranny Overholt; he and Ireland put themselves out to entertain her, and by evening some of her perturbation had vanished. Nobody wanted to go to bed early that night, and Martin Quest suggested that they stay up all night.

Quest said, "If we stay awake, and keep our heads and stay together, it's impossible for anything to happen. Isn't that so, Pat?"

"Well, it's about as good insurance as you can get under the circumstances, I imagine."

"It's settled then. We'll stick right here in the living room until daylight. Anybody gets bored and wants to go to sleep, he can pick his spot—chairs, davenports, or the floor."

Jewell Northrup told Campbell plaintively that she had searched high and low for the rod, but it simply wasn't anywhere. It had completely disappeared. Campbell said, "Well, don't worry about it. You can look again tomorrow if we don't find it."

By nine o'clock an air of subdued and false gaiety had gradually been adopted as the most generally approved method of deportment. Bess and Eilers played gin rummy with Quest and Ireland until Bess began to grow drowsy, and Quest kidded her about being an early bird. The Northrups, Overholt and Sally and Francie were playing twenty questions. The radio was turned on full blast and no one was listening to it. Eilers whispered to Campbell that there'd be no need of the horse bell tonight.

The detective strolled around the room, watching and listening, his attention divided.

It was nearly nine-thirty when Grannat came to the door, caught Campbell's eye, and beckoned with his head. Campbell followed the butler into the hall.

Grannat was upset. "Would you come this way, sir? Cook is about to have a fit. She says there are prowlers in the house."

Campbell followed the butler into the kitchen, where Sophronia was standing by the stove peering at a coffee cake she was baking for breakfast. She straightened, closed the oven door, and sighed in relief at sight of Campbell.

"Mistah Campbell, sah! Somethin's wrong around heah. I done heared footsteps in the hall, and when I goes in there to look, ain't nobody there. Anybody that leery about bein' seen ain't got no business in this house!"

"What hall, Phrony?"

"The back hall, sah. Thoo that door right ovah yondah."

The detective walked over to the door and stood close, with his ear almost against the panels. He heard nothing. He asked in a whisper, "What rooms open off this hall, Phrony?"

"The storage closet, sah. The linen closet. The kitchen heah. The main hall. The back stairs. The service po'ch. And that's all. What's anybody prowlin' round heah fo'? Scared me half outen my wits, Mistah Campbell."

Campbell said softly, "Shhh, Phrony! Listen." He heard footsteps now, moving cautiously along the linoleum on the back hall floor. He whispered, "Maybe you weren't quite quick enough, Phrony." While the steps were still sounding, he turned the knob and jerked the door wide open.

The lights in the hall were subdued, but the figure caught unaware, too far from any convenient hiding place, looked dark and tall, as if frozen to the spot. The glow of the bulbs gleamed on chestnut brown hair, and clear-coffee eyes stared at Campbell out of a beautiful and startled face.

The detective said, "Well, Miss Taylor! I've been expecting you. Come in!"

She shrugged and started to move slowly toward him. "I might as well. Why do you have to be so devilishly vigilant? If you'd kept out of this, I could have gone on playing hide and seek with everybody else very successfully."

"How long have you been around?" Campbell asked.

She paused in the doorway, looking past him at the gaping Phrony and the old butler. "I moved in before daylight this morning. Walked from the Logus bus, with a flashlight for dark spots in the road."

Campbell said, "I saw your light in the canyon. Come on in and sit down. If you've been on the premises since last night, you must be hungry."

"I could eat a house cat, raw." The girl walked to the nearest chair and sat down, clasping between her hands the large brown pocketbook she carried.

"So here's your prowler, Phrony," Campbell said. "This is the cook, Nina, and the butler. Phrony, Grannat, this is Miss Nina Taylor. I think Miss Taylor was looking for me, and trying to avoid discovery by anyone else."

The girl smiled at the cook's brown interested face. "Hello, Phrony. I hope you can cook as good as you look. I'm famished."

Sophronia changed like a weather vane, from wary suspicion to a beaming smile. "Yas, ma'm! I sho' can cook. You just sit up there to the table, and I'll fotch you food. Heh, heh! Ain't got no house cat, though, miss."

"I can get along without it." Her gaze turned to the thin old butler. "I'm glad to know you, Grannat. You won't let anybody else know I'm around, will you? I'm here on business, in a way; Mr. Campbell knows what I mean. I'll hang around with you and Phrony at the back of the house, if you'll let me. You'll keep it dark about me, won't you?"

Grannat summoned his best bow. "Yes, indeed, miss. Any friend of Mr. Campbell will always receive our full attention and co-operation."

"A friend?" An impish grin flashed at Campbell, mocking him. "Well, the word has covered more sins than mine, Grannat. Do you suppose you could find me a drink somewhere? I could use one."

"Yes indeed. What would you like, miss?"

"A whisky sour, if it isn't too much trouble. With rye, if you have any."

Campbell stood looking down at the girl without much

amusement in his eyes. "Just what did you come here for, Nina? I think I know, but suppose you tell me. And don't be backward on account of Sophronia or Grannat. The staff knows more about what's going on here than anybody else."

"I came to keep an eye on Bess, of course." The anger flashed again. "I don't intend to let her get too far out of hand. If you care to look in this pocketbook you'll find out what makes it so heavy. Thirty-eight caliber, *and* loaded."

The detective said abruptly, "Naomi Andross was murdered last night, Nina. Most of the folks in the other room don't know it yet. It might be dangerous to go snooping around the back halls in the dark."

"Dangerous for anybody who tried any funny business around me, yes. Don't worry about me, Mr. Campbell—don't give it a thought!" The low voice was mocking. "I'm not going to bother anybody, if nobody bothers me, and I'll keep out from under foot. But Bess can only get about so far without me, and she knows it."

She turned her head, as Sophronia approached the table with a tray; a tray laden with steaming coffee, a jug of cream, fresh hot coffee cake and a pot of strawberry jam. There was also a plate of cold baked ham and candied sweet potatoes.

"Heavens, Phrony! Where did all that come from? You're a wizard!" The girl sniffed hungrily. She raised her eyes as Grannat came up with her drink. "Thanks, Grannat. Man, how I need that! You'd better sit down and have a bite with me, Campbell. I can't eat all this. Phrony's eyes are bigger than my stomach."

The cook giggled and set the last dishes off the tray.

Campbell said, "I have other fish to fry. I'll leave you to Phrony and Grannat for the present."

He went back to the big living room, but he did not enter it: he stopped in the doorway, surveying the occupants. Someone had shut off the radio, games had palled, Francie was reading a book to Sally Mace, and the Northrups were conversing quietly with Ranny Overholt and Martin Quest. Ireland was walking around the room with a drink in his hand. Bess was asleep on a divan, with Eilers sprawled in a chair a few feet away. George Landis was sitting a little way back of the divan where Bess slept, alertly keeping an eye on everybody in the room.

The policeman's eyes met Campbell's as the detective appeared in the doorway, and Landis queried, "Did you want something, Pat?"

"Yes. I want Eilers. Need to compare a few notes. We won't be long. Don't let anybody leave this room, on any pretext whatever, George, until we come back. If anybody decides he wants to change his mind and go to bed, he'll simply have to wait."

Landis nodded, and as Eilers deserted the chair near Bess, the policeman moved into it. Landis said, "I'll see that they stay put."

The detective went along the hall and up the stairs, with Eilers close behind. The two men went into their suite and switched on the lights, and Campbell said, "Let's see what you got."

Eilers gestured toward a small table at which he had been working while Bess was in her own room. On the table were seven of the colored plastic glasses in which Grannat had served the spiked milk at breakfast. By the glasses was the small paper doily that had been on the plate under Eilers' dry toast. The doily was turned over. On its under side Grannat had written in small, neat script:

Mr. Northrup—pink	*Mr. Quest—lettuce green*
Mrs. Northrup—purple	*Mr. Overholt—yellow*
Miss Mace—pale blue	*Miss Dunham—bottle green*
Mr. Ireland—lavender	*Miss Holloway—red*

Campbell asked, "Good prints?"

"Practically perfect. Identified Naomi's prints from objects no one but she would have handled. The prints in Naomi's room were her own, Jewell Northrup's, Ike Northrup's and Francie Dunham's."

"Where'd you find the Dunham girl's prints?"

"On the mirror, on some of the toilette articles, on the inside doorknob over all others, and on the outside doorknob under yours."

Campbell said, "Hmmm. So Francie was the last one in that room, and came out of the room before I tried the knob to see whether the door was locked—after I saw that Naomi's light had been turned out."

"I don't see how there can be any other answer."

Campbell said, thinking aloud, "If she ducked into Naomi's room at some time when I'd stopped in here for a minute, and ducked out again when she found Nomy wasn't there, she might have run into the killer—no, he'd have ducked himself when he heard her at the door."

"She admit to you that she'd been out of her room at any time for a few minutes?"

"She did not. I'll take it up with her later." Campbell gave his assistant a summation of the facts he'd gleaned in his questioning. "Ike's story sounds pretty straight. He says they went down to the glass house to pick the night-blooming cereus flowers, then came back past the pool. And Naomi said when she was dying that she'd been past the pool. She simply wasn't wasting breath to explain that she was with Ike, or probably she thought it wasn't pertinent. The only thing she wanted to get over to me then was her hearing the quarrel."

"You anywhere near closing in, Pat?"

"I'll have our murderer by morning, kid. Things are a little hazy in spots, but they'll clear."

"Still look like anybody's party?"

"I'm afraid it does, granted that anyone could have gotten out of and back into his room by window and ladder. Outside of that, it's narrowing down. We know now that Francie was in Naomi's room. We know that Ranny Overholt came out of his room and went downstairs to get a bottle of whisky. We know that Quest admits being the last one out of the pool enclosure, leaving Wark there alive and unhurt—so Quest says. We know that somebody deliberately went into the pool area right after Ransome left the pool filled, and opened the sluice gate so the pool would be nearly empty when Wark wanted to go out to swim that night. By the way, Rick; Bess' roommate is here."

"The hell she is! Where?"

"In the kitchen, under Grannat's eagle eye. Filling up on Phrony's cooking. Well, you'd better be getting back to your watchdog job. I have some snooping to do. Here, take the keys, in case you need 'em while I'm on the prowl."

"Think your ruse of pretending Naomi's alive is going to pay off?" Eilers took the keys and dropped them into his pocket.

"I think so," Campbell answered.

The two men went out of the room, locked the door and went on downstairs. Eilers returned to the big living room. Campbell went quietly up the hall, through the small lounge, and out into the patio via the side door.

15

HE WENT DIAGONALLY ACROSS the patio to the servants' wing, knocked on the first door he came to and asked for Thibault. One of the maids answered the door, and told him Thibault was in the third room beyond hers. Campbell went on to Thibault's door and knocked again. There was a light in the room, and Thibault appeared without delay, peering into the night, smiling quickly when he saw the big detective waiting there.

The little man said warmly, "Mr. Campbell! Come in, sir!"

Campbell said, "No, you come out, Thibault. I want a little assistance from you."

"Yes, sir. Be with you immediately." He turned his reading lamp low, came out and closed the door. "What can I do to help you, sir?"

Campbell gestured toward the garage. "Would there be a ladder over there, or anywhere handy, long enough to get up on the roof with?"

"Yes, sir. There's an extension ladder in the garden house."

"Good. Let's get it and set it for the roof."

Thibault led the way to the garden house, Campbell's flashlight illuminating the path. Thibault felt in an urn standing near the door of the garden house, produced a key and unlocked the padlock on the door.

Campbell asked, "Are the out buildings always padlocked at night, Thibault?"

"Oh, yes, sir. There have been prowlers about at times."

The ladder was light in weight, and Thibault protested that he could carry it. Campbell smiled down at the small man and didn't make the mistake of insisting that he take it. Thibault locked the door, and slipped the padlock key in his pocket.

Campbell said, "We'll go around on the other side of the house, and I'll show you where to set up the ladder."

They went back to the house and started around the back of the large building. Campbell led the way, and called a halt below the window looking out from Francie Dunham's bathroom. He told Thibault to set up the ladder, and stood waiting, playing his flash idly about, on the ground and at the bases of the near-by trees. The flash beam caught on something that gleamed pale yellow in the thick foliage of a large cypress.

Campbell said, "Hold it a minute, Thibault. I was hoping we might run across something like this."

Thibault came up beside him, to look curiously where the flash beam pointed. "A bamboo fish pole, sir! How did it get caught in the tree? What's it doing there?"

Campbell said, "I think I can guess, Thibault. Set the ladder up here first, and fetch the pole down. Take it by the tip, so as not to mar any fingerprints that might be on it—that *will* be on it, if I'm guessing right."

Thibault said, "Yes, sir." He set the ladder up against the tree, and brought down the fish pole, dangling it carefully by the end.

Campbell took it by the tip of the handle, and pushed it under the shrub at the far end of the patio, while Thibault set the ladder up for the roof.

Thibault said, "What am I to look for on the roof, sir?"

"A curtain rod, Thibault. Somebody up there in that bathroom, late last night or early this morning, had to get rid of a curtain rod quick. It was a foot and a half long, too long to be hidden easily in any clothing. There was no place in the bathroom to hide it. I think the person had no opportunity to return it to the supply closet off the back hall on the first floor. He wouldn't have tossed it to the ground where it would be found. The smart thing to do would be drop it on the roof close under the window, until he had time to retrieve it and put it in the closet."

"One of those brass rods with the strawberry end, sir?"

"That's the kind, Thibault. The small size. Hurry along and see if it's up there. Here, take the flashlight."

"Yes, sir." Again Thibault went up the ladder. For a few moments he was out of sight, and only the glow of the flashlight showed dimly where he turned the beam down upon the roof. Then he was coming down the ladder for the second time with something dangling from his hand. "It was right there, Mr. Campbell. Close against the wall. But what's the fish pole got to do with it?"

"The killer wanted to hide the weapon in the tube it had come out of, Thibault. But Grannat had placed another rod in the tube. This is the one Grannat brought up. The killer got rid of it fast, by dropping it out of the window onto the roof. But it wouldn't drop so it couldn't be seen. And it couldn't be seen. I looked. So someone had to take something in there, when the girls were out of the room, and maneuver the rod close to the wall out of sight. That's what he used the fish pole for. He did about the only thing he could do with the pole to get rid of it. He speared it down into that cypress tree. He didn't think it would be found there. And he couldn't wipe his fingerprints off it after it was in the air, Thibault."

"No, I should say not, sir! That fish pole's a direct clue to the murderer, isn't it?"

"Well, it could be, if I'm guessing right. We have to do a lot of guessing about these things sometimes, and regrettably often our guesses are a mile off the track."

"Anything else I can do now, sir?"

"No. That's all right now, and thanks very much, Thibault. Don't say a word to anyone about this little excursion. Return the ladder to the garden house. Go back to your room and sit tight."

Thibault went away with the ladder. The detective returned to the patio, retrieved the fish pole, then went into the house via the door into the back hall, and up to the second floor by the back stairs, carrying fish pole and curtain rod into his own suite. He laid them carefully down on the bed, and went back to the living room.

He told Eilers in a low aside, "Couple of things on the bed to be dusted. Make it snappy. I'll wait for you here." Eilers went out of the living room, and Landis moved over to sit beside Campbell.

"How's it coming, Pat?"

"We're getting there, George."

"Got your man spotted yet?"

"Not quite. There are some conflicting angles that have me held up for the time being, but I'll straighten them out."

Jewell Northrup rose from her chair and came over to the detective. "Mr. Campbell, this sitting up all night is proving too much for me, and Ike is about ready to pass out. I think we all ought to change our minds and go to bed."

"That's all right with me, Mrs. Northrup. What's the consensus?"

Quentin Ireland said with a yawn, "Consensus is in the affirmative. Any dissenters?" No one voiced any objection, and sleep-heavy eyes looked to the detective for direction.

Campbell said, "All right, then, the ayes have it. You will go up in the order I name. Officer Landis will accompany each of you to your door. He will take your key off the dresser, lock your door on the outside, and come back with your keys in his pocket. I had a set of keys on a ring last night, George, but I turned them over to Eilers. If you need to get into a room in a hurry, you don't want to fish around among a lot of loose keys in your pocket. As soon as Eilers comes down, he'll give you the bunch on the ring. You can leave the loose keys in our suite later."

Francie Dunham asked, "Couldn't Officer Landis go up for the keys now? I'm practically dead on my feet."

"No," Campbell said. "Eilers is busy, and I don't want him bothered. It won't take him long."

Sally Mace looked at him with a frown. "You had the keys last night? Why? We never lock our doors here. We never even have any keys in the doors."

Campbell said. "So I understand. I got the keys from Naomi."

"What for?" Sally persisted. "None of our doors was locked."

Martin Quest put in impatiently, "Don't ask so many questions, Sally. Our doors certainly were locked. I know. I tried mine."

Campbell looked at him. "So? I don't remember your mentioning that when I was talking to you, Mart."

"I didn't think of it. It was of no importance. I just thought I'd go down and get another bottle of whisky. Ranny'd gone to bed and I was reading. When I found the door locked, I guessed you'd done it for our own safety, forgot about the whisky and went to bed."

Campbell said, "I see. Okay."

Jewell Northrup's slightly protruding blue eyes blinked at the detective. "I don't know as I like the idea of being locked in my room. Suppose somebody tried to crawl in the window?"

Ike roused in his chair. "Don't be a sap, Jewell. You wouldn't like the idea of somebody poking a sharpened curtain rod into your guts either, would you?"

Jewell shivered, and a spasm of pain passed over her face.

Campbell knew she was thinking of Naomi. He said quietly, "No one is going to crawl through any windows. No one crawled through any windows last night. All the ladders are kept under lock and key in the garden house. I didn't know that until this evening. Nobody could get to any of the upstairs windows without a ladder. Unless he shinnied up the patio balcony supports, and then the only window he could get into would be a hall window."

Jewell said, "Oh. I never thought about that." Then she leaned close to Campbell and whispered, "I haven't found a trace of the—you know. I haven't been much good, have I?"

"You've kept yourself from thinking too hard," the detective said. "That was worth doing, Mrs. Northrup."

She started to make some answer, then stopped as she saw Eilers come into the room. She stepped back, as the assistant approached Campbell.

Campbell said, "Give George the keys. Everybody wants to go to bed. They all know they're to be locked in tonight."

Eilers handed the ring of keys over to Landis, and the officer looked at them in close scrutiny. The name of each suite or room was stamped on the shank of the brass key that fitted its door. Campbell said, "Jewell, you and Ike go up first. Stay close to Landis until you're inside your door."

The Northrups went out, with Landis close behind.

Francie Dunham said, "May we go next?"

The detective nodded. "Certainly. You and Sally next. Then Mart and Ranny. Ireland last."

All impulse to talk faded, then. Eilers again sat down near the divan where Bess slept. Landis saw the last person safe inside a locked door and came back into the living room to return the keys to Campbell.

The detective said, "Keep them in your pocket. You're to patrol that upper hall tonight. Eilers will be in our suite with Bess. Keep the connecting door wide open and the night light on, Rick. I'll be here and there. Find anything?"

"Yep. Good clear prints on the fish pole—Ranny Overholt's. And on the brass strawberry of the curtain rod—Grannat's. These were a little smudged, as if someone had gripped the rod with gloves or a handkerchief after Grannat had handled it."

Campbell sighed. "That's another thing I was afraid of. Well, let's wake Bess and get everybody on the job." He rose, stepped to the couch, and laid a hand on Bess' shoulder. She roused quickly, looking up at him, then sat erect. The detective said, "Everyone else has gone to bed, Bess. You'd better do the same."

She shrank a little, her small face tired and worried. "I'm scared. I wish I could go home."

Campbell said, "You'll go up to your room with Landis and Eilers. Landis will patrol the hall all night. Eilers will be sitting where he can keep watch on you. Nothing can possibly hurt you, no one can possibly get to you, if you continue to obey orders. Run along. You've nothing to worry about, and I'm going to be pretty busy from here out."

Bess asked timidly, "What time is it?"

"It's past midnight. Time for you to be in bed long ago. Get moving, Rick."

The girl went reluctantly out of the room with Eilers holding one of her arms and Landis lightly gripping the other. Eilers was talking to her, joking with her, as they disappeared through the doorway into the hall, but he was having a hard time coaxing a smile to her face.

The detective thought, She's feeling trapped; she looks and acts trapped. She'd leave this place in nothing flat, if she had the chance. She'll just have to take it and wait.

He went out of the living room, down the hall toward the kitchen, feeling again the chill of the night air sweeping down the canyon and through the house.

16

HE PAUSED IN THE kitchen doorway, smiling at the scene that greeted him. Sophronia was standing by the table, a spatula in one hand and a platter in the other, sliding onto a plate a wedge of strawberry shortcake smothered with whipped cream. Grannat was standing a few feet away watching the proceedings with an interested eye.

Campbell moved on into the room and shut the door behind him. "My God, Nina, are you still eating? What a digestion! How do you think you're going to do any sleeping on top of all that food?"

She looked up at him, her flashing eyes and her full lips smiling. "Oh, but I slept most of the day, under the trees, waiting for dark so I could sneak into the house. And the minute I set foot inside, Phrony cocks her big rabbit ears and catches me cold. I don't close an eye again now until that will is read."

"You're keeping Grannat and Phrony up. They should have been in bed hours ago."

Grannat said, "Oh, no, sir! None of us feels much like sleeping. The rest of the staff are all in their rooms, but I doubt that any of them is asleep."

The detective sat down at the table. "I could use a piece of that shortcake, Phrony. I'm a little hollow at the belt line." He said to the butler, "I noticed that the service wing is all lit up. That your doing, Grannat?"

"Well, in a way, sir. I told them they could go to their quarters, but they might as well stay dressed and ready for anything. None of us has ever been in a house where there was murder done, before, sir. And with the will reading and all tomorrow, we're all sort of on edge, as you might say."

"I shouldn't wonder." Campbell turned to his shortcake with gustatory anticipation. "You'd better turn that gun over to me, Nina. It's liable to get you into trouble."

"It may help to keep Bess out of trouble," the girl said slowly. "That's why I followed her here. She's always depended on me. She's likely any time to begin to feel lost without me and want to go home. She mustn't go home. She must stay right here and see it through."

Campbell looked up at the butler curiously. "Do you know who Miss Taylor is talking about, Grannat? Did you know anything about Elizabeth Anne?"

"Oh, yes indeed, sir. I came down from Seattle with Mr. Andross, you know. I entered Mr. Andross' employ just a little while after you left Seattle. I was practically his whole staff then. I acted as messenger the last few times he sent word to the first Mrs. Andross, before she disappeared from Seattle."

The detective said quickly, "Then how did she manage to get away so quietly that he didn't discover it for months? I mean, if you were keeping in close touch with her for him."

"I was very sorry for the first Mrs. Andross, sir," the butler said a little stiffly. "I was very fond of little Miss Mary. She was a lovely child. Mr. Andross was trying to persuade the first Mrs. Andross to accept an allowance for the little girl, but she was very bitter. I couldn't say that I blame her much, sir. She told me she was going away, she said she couldn't stand to stay there any longer, with him continually keeping at her that way. She begged me not to let him know she had left for at least six months, until the trail had gone cold, as you might say, sir. So I told him they kept telling me at her apartment house that she wasn't in. He never knew the difference. I didn't feel that I was being disloyal to Mr. Andross. All she wanted was to be left in peace with the little girl. I figured she had her rights, sir."

"Yes, I think she did." Campbell pushed aside his empty plate. "I consider that you acted very admirably, Grannat. No, Phrony! No more. I haven't a cast iron stomach, like Miss Taylor here." He said to the butler, "Then you placed the young lady who came with me as Bess Holloway?"

The butler looked levelly into his eyes, half smiling. "I knew who she was supposed to be, and I knew she *wasn't* who she was supposed to be, sir."

"I'd take it, with your talking so freely in front of Phrony, that the rest of the staff know about Mary Elizabeth Andross?"

"Yes, sir. I told them after the master died. In case you found her before the will was read, I thought it was better for them to know, sir. Any of us would be very happy to be installed here in the Canyon House with Miss Mary, sir."

Campbell rose from his chair. "You'll probably all end by being installed here in the Canyon House, Grannat." He looked at the girl sitting erect and politely at attention beside the table. "There's another whole wing of this house unoccupied, Nina. Sure you don't want Grannat to call one of the maids and have a room readied for you? What are you going to do with yourself between now and one o'clock this afternoon? It's already Tuesday, you know."

"You needn't worry about me, Mr. Campbell. I'll stay out of

sight, and I won't make any trouble for anyone. But if Bess gets scared out of her wits, if she begins asking to go home, I want her to know I am here. I'll go to bed, if you'll let me go to Bess' room."

Campbell looked fixedly into her eyes. "I think you'd better stay away from Bess, don't you? I understand the whole set-up now, and I think we've had enough murder. This business of snatching oranges out of the gutter, and rooms not fit for dogs to whelp in, not to speak of alley basement entrances, was just a little heavy pressure to gain sympathy, wasn't it?"

"That's all."

"But there had been real hard days, real hunger, and I would guess that the lack of jobs was simply an inability to hold a job for any length of time. Am I right?"

"Yes." The girl nodded her shining chestnut head. "That's right. And no relatives to turn to. No friends."

Campbell said, "Yes. I understand. I really do, you know. So suppose you trust me fully, and let's bury the hatchet. We'll see Bess through together, shall we?"

Without a word, she handed him her pocketbook. He took the gun out of it, put the gun in his pocket, and returned the purse to her. He said to the butler, "I have to ask a favor of you and Phrony, Grannat. I hope you won't mind too much."

Grannat said, "Anything we can do, sir. Gladly."

Sophronia said, "Yas, sah, Mist' Campbell. We's right on the job, sah."

"Then, whatever you know, from here on out, keep it strictly to yourselves and don't even talk about it to each other. Mary Andross' life may depend on it," the detective said quietly. "Lock all the doors and the windows into the kitchen and pantry, pull down those blinds, and stay right here in the kitchen with Miss Taylor until you hear further from me.

Don't let anyone in here but me, and don't any of you go out of the room for anything whatever. There's a toilet on the service porch for general use, isn't there?"

"Yes, sir," Grannat said. "And I'll close and bolt the outside door to the service porch."

Campbell said, "That ought to do it. Lock all the other doors leading into the back hall. If Miss Taylor has to go out, you and Phrony accompany her to the door, wait for her and bring her back. Lock the door into the kitchen again after you've come in. If all this seems a bit drastic, remember that I'm trying to prevent another murder. And I *will* prevent it if my orders are obeyed to the letter."

"Yes, sir. I realize that, sir." The old butler held his head up stiffly. "We'd do anything to preserve Miss Mary's safety, sir. I'm happier than I can say that she has been found. She looks very much as she did when she was a little girl, sir. I think I'd have known her anywhere. It was very clever of you, bringing her here under another name that way, if I may say so, sir."

"Well, thanks, Grannat! We both thought a lot of Wark Andross, Grannat. The last thing we can do for him is to see that Mary comes into her own. Maybe she'll discard the Elizabeth and take back the Mary when she adopts her real name of Andross. For Wark's sake, I hope so. She was always Mary to him."

"And to me, sir. You may depend on Sophronia and me with absolute ease of mind, Mr. Campbell. We will keep Miss Taylor under strict guard until further orders from you."

"Good! Well, I'll move along. Thanks for the swell short-cake, Phrony."

"Sho' are welcome, Mist' Campbell, sah. Always mo' where that came from."

"I'll remember that." The detective paused before going out of the kitchen, to look back at the girl sitting by the table. She had taken a pack of cigarettes out of her pocketbook, and was just in the act of lighting one. Over the flame she watched him, smiling, waiting for his parting words. Campbell said, "Just take it easy, Nina. I'll be seeing you around." He went out and closed the door.

Almost immediately Grannat turned the key in the lock. Campbell turned away, satisfied, and went on up the hall.

The entire big house was almost without a sound now, chilly and still in the night of the canyon. The detective went up the stairs to the second floor hall, to find everything dark and quiet there, the little balls on the pull chains glowing, the faint whisper of Landis' feet on the hall carpet coming toward him.

Campbell said softly, "It's me, George. Everything okay?"

"Right as a trivet." Landis stopped close by, and went on in a low voice. "Quest had his radio on for a while, some late news broadcasts and speeches. Wasn't loud, but I wanted to be able to hear any little untoward noises. I finally told him to shut it off. Haven't heard a peep out of anybody else. All of 'em dead to the world the minute they hit the pillow but Quest, I guess. I don't know what the hell was keeping him awake. Guilty conscience, maybe?"

Campbell said dryly, "Could be. Mmmm—listen, George. Do you hear anything?"

The two men stood silent, waiting for a sound. There was nothing.

Landis whispered, "What did you hear?"

"I can't be sure. It sounded like a dog whimpering. You seen any dogs around here?"

Landis said, "Nary a pup."

They stood listening again. Then they both heard it. It did sound like a dog whimpering, in fright or in pain.

Campbell said abruptly, "I don't think that's a dog."

"Shall we go down and investigate?" Landis asked.

"I'll go down and investigate, George. You stick right here until you hear from me." The detective wheeled and went toward the stairs, and took the descent three treads at a time, his flashlight playing ahead of him.

When he reached the lower hall, he stopped and listened again. He heard nothing more of the odd whimpering cry here. He went on out of the house, via the front door, the flashlight extinguished now. On the front porch he paused again. The cry came clearly now, subdued. It seemed to emanate from some spot near the patio. Campbell leaped off the porch and rounded the corner of the main wing, went through the archway between the service wing and the main house into the patio. The odd whimpering cry ended in a rasping gasp as he stopped just inside the archway.

He pressed the slide on his flash, and swept the beam about the patio flagstones. Within ten feet of him Bess lay huddled on her side, dressed for the street, her eyes staring and half open, bulging. Her tongue protruded, and some kind of white rag was tied tightly about her throat. He plunged toward her, went down on his knees, set the flashlight on a flagstone, took out his knife and cut through the white rag at the back of her neck. As he pulled the rag away, he saw that it was a torn strip of strong linen sheeting. He thrust knife and rag into his pocket, picked up the flashlight and turned it upon the girl's face. The eyes stared glassily into the light. He laid his fingers on her pulse. There was no heart beat.

He began cursing under his breath as he lifted the small

body into his arms and carried her swiftly into the living room. He did not immediately notify anyone else. He knew it was no use, but he tried artificial respiration. Nothing was any use. The girl was dead. He stood for a moment looking down at her, his jaw set, his eyes angry.

Then he lifted her into his arms again and went with her up the stairs. Landis was waiting at the head of the flight, and the detective whispered, "Go along to my door and knock. I've got Bess here—strangled. How the hell did she ever get past you and Rick?"

Landis gasped. "By God, she didn't! Nobody's come out into this hall. *Nobody!*"

Campbell said, "Well, get that door of mine open fast. See what's happened to Rick."

Landis went ahead to the door of *Quatro* and knocked. There was no answer.

Campbell said, "Try the door. Unlock it yourself. Kick it down if you have to. It doesn't matter if you rouse the whole house, now."

Landis tried the knob. The door was locked. He took a small pair of long-nosed pincers from his pocket, worked the key about in the lock and poked it out onto the floor inside the room. "Thank God for old-fashioned door locks in country houses," he muttered, as he inserted in the lock the *Quatro* key on the ring Eilers had given him, unlocked the door and flung it open.

Campbell lunged past him into the room. Landis followed him in and shut the door. The shaded lamps were on, but Eilers was nowhere in sight. Campbell laid the girl's body on the bed, and went on into her room. The lights were off here, and he found the nearest button with his flashlight, turned the current on.

Eilers lay on the rug beside the girl's bed, his fair hair matted with oozing blood. The detective bent over him. Somebody had hit his assistant a hard blow on the skull with some object sharp enough to make a nasty gash in the scalp.

Campbell picked him up and placed him on the girl's bed, then looked at Landis. "He's not dead. I don't think he's even badly hurt. He's unconscious and may stay that way for a while. I'll bandage his head, and get Thibault to come in here and stay with him. He's in no immediate danger, but I don't want him left alone. And you and I have work to do."

Landis said, "I'll go get Thibault while you fix Eilers up."

"Fine! Do that! Fourth door down in the servants' wing. Don't tell him anything till you get him up here, just tell him I want him. As long as we didn't have to wake the house up, let's leave things quiet for a few minutes."

Landis said, "Okay. I'll be right back with Thibault."

The detective cleaned and bandaged Eilers' head, then he began looking around for the weapon that had been used on his assistant. He hadn't far to look. It had been tossed back under the bed. It was a heavy cold cream jar, with blood smears showing on the sharp edge of its base. Campbell rolled it out, picked it up by the top and set it on a tray on the dresser. He was just turning back toward the bed, when Landis came in with Thibault.

Thibault looked down at Eilers. "Will he be all right, sir?"

"Oh, yes. He's not really hurt. Just banged up a little." Campbell gestured toward a chair. "Stay here and keep an eye on him, in case he wakes up and wants anything."

Thibault shuddered. "That poor girl out there on your bed, sir. She looks awful."

Campbell said, "Strangled people usually do. Thibault, I wanted to ask you—meant to ask you several times, kept forgetting—but that key to the grille gate in the fence about the big pool at the Beverly Hills place. Would Wark have had that key on him while he was inside the enclosure?"

"No, sir. It was the custom for whoever went in there to swim to leave the key on the inside of the lock, as a matter of convenience. Then one always knew where it was, and it was handy when you were ready to go out. So it would have been inside the gate in the lock, sir."

"How did you get in when you went looking for Wark, then?"

"When he didn't answer, I knew something was wrong, sir. I got a ladder and climbed over the fence. It was all I could do."

"And the key was in the lock inside?"

"No, sir. It had been, but it had fallen out onto the tile. I had to turn on the nearest floodlight to find it. That was odd, too, because you could hardly slam that gate hard enough to make the key fall out."

"I don't think it fell out, Thibault. Whoever closed that gate last was in a hurry to get out of there, took the key with him from sheer force of habit, then thought in time that the key shouldn't be outside in the box when Wark was still in the enclosure. Besides, he didn't want to make it easy for anyone to get in too soon. But the gate was already shut, he didn't want to take time to open it again, so he poked the key through the grille." Campbell turned to Landis. "We're ready for the showdown, George. Go on down to the living room, turn all the lights on, and wait there."

"You're rousing the house now?"

"That's right. There are three doors into the living room, if you've noticed: one at the front of the room letting into the hall near the front door, one in the middle of the room opening into the hall across from the little lounge, and one at the rear of the room giving onto the hall at the foot of the stairs. Shut and lock the ones at the front and in the middle, and put the keys in your pocket. Leave the one at the back near the stairs standing open."

"You got the goods on your killer now, Pat?"

"No. I doubt that I ever would have it. He's too slick to leave any opening or any tracks. I'll just have to beat him down."

Landis said, "Okay. I'll be standing by." He went out of the suite and down the stairs.

Campbell said to Thibault, "If Eilers comes out of it and feels like it, you two come on down to the living room."

"Yes, sir."

The detective went out of the suite, turned left to the next door and rapped on it. He had to knock three times before Francie Dunham answered drowsily. "Who's there?"

"Campbell. Get dressed and come down to the living room immediately, both of you."

"Oh. Yes. All right." The voice was instantly wide awake. He heard her speaking to Sally Mace as he crossed the hall to the door of *Tres*.

He heard the bubbling snore inside the room. It kept on after he knocked, then Ike Northrup's voice inquired impatiently, "Who is it? What do you want?"

"It's Campbell, Ike. You and your wife get down to the living room, pronto."

He went on, toward the end of the hall, not waiting for Northrup's answer, to knock at *Cinco*. Ranny woke, answered the second knock, feet sounded on the floor and a hand tried the doorknob. Ranny said, "Hell, I forgot we were locked in. Anything wrong, Pat?"

Campbell said, "I want you and Mart down in the living room. I'll unlock the doors when you're all dressed, and you can all come down together."

"I'll probably have a hell of a time getting Mart up," Ranny Overholt said. "He always takes a sleeping pill when he's upset. But I'll jar him out of it."

Campbell crossed the hall again to rap at the door of *Seis.* Ireland answered immediately. "Yes? What's wanted?"

The detective said, "It's Campbell, Ireland. I want everybody down in the living room right away."

Ireland said, "Glad to hear it. Couldn't get to sleep after I turned in. Wakeful as a cat. Be right down, Campbell."

The detective went downstairs to the kitchen and knocked there.

Grannat's voice said, "Is that you, Mr. Campbell?"

"Right, Grannat. When I ring for you, bring Miss Taylor and come into the living room, please."

"Yes, sir."

Campbell turned away, went into the living room himself, to find all lights on, and Landis lounging against the locked door at the front of the room. "Let me have the keys, George. They should be ready to come down now."

Landis handed over the keys. "You don't want 'em to realize these two doors are locked, eh?"

"No. We've got to ram this through before somebody else disobeys orders and there's another killing. This is the damnedest runaround, George. Hell's bells! I can't even dig up an acceptable motive!" The detective went out of the room with the key ring swinging from one finger, and on up the stairs.

He went on to the far end of the hall, unlocked Ireland's door first, and waited for him to come out. Then he opened the door across the hall from Ireland. Ranny Overholt, in green-striped pajamas, was sitting on the edge of Quest's bed, shaking him by the shoulder. Quest was sitting beside him, humped over, and he looked up at the detective groggily, a protesting grimace on his ugly face.

"Good God, man, don't I even get a chance to sleep when I take a pill?"

Campbell said quietly, "Bess has been murdered, Mart."

That did it. Quest's eyes flew wide, and he got to his feet, swaying a little. "My dressing gown, Rann. Get your own on. Where to, Pat?"

The detective said, "Follow along."

Overholt fetched the dressing gowns, and all four men went on along the hall, Campbell unlocking the other doors and adding the Northrups and the girls to the group. Then they went on down to the living room, Campbell shepherding them like a drove of startled sheep.

17

I<small>NSIDE THE ROOM</small>, <small>THE</small> detective directed them all to seats toward the front of the room near Landis. He himself stopped a few feet inside the room's rear door, and stood facing the company, his gaze going from one to another, scrutinizing expressions.

He heard steps behind him, and half turned, to see Thibault coming through the doorway. Eilers, at Thibault's elbow, was alert and chipper in spite of an aching and bandaged head.

Campbell said, "Hold it. That's a good spot for you."

Thibault and Eilers halted and stood filling and guarding the open doorway.

Eilers said, "I won't have to dust that cold cream jar. I know who hit me. You knew it was Bess herself, of course."

The detective said, "It couldn't be anybody else. No one could possibly have entered that room, with you sitting there watching the windows with a gun in your pocket."

Eilers said, "Check. If anybody had showed at a window, I'd have shot first and asked questions afterwards."

Jewell Northrup's voice rose, sharp with dismay. "What is all this? What's the matter?"

Quest said thickly, still groggy from the sleeping draught, "Shut up! Everybody keep still. Bess has been murdered."

Campbell said to Eilers, "How the hell did she ever get a chance at you?"

Eilers made a disgusted face. "The poor dumb kid was scared half to death. I felt like spanking her, yet I couldn't help being sorry for her. She started crying, saying she wanted to go home, and asked me to come in and sit by her. She was sitting on the edge of the bed. I went over and sat down by her and patted her hand. Told her to cheer up, there were only a few hours to go. She was quick as a cat. She had that damn cold cream jar hidden on the bed beside her, under the edge of her skirt."

Campbell said, "And she whammed you with it before you realized what she was up to."

"You said it! She whammed two or three times. She knocked me cuckoo, all right, but she couldn't hit hard enough to do any real damage."

"She could have if she'd kept on hitting long enough," Campbell said dryly. "It was your salvation that she wanted to get out as fast as possible and didn't take time to do a good job of it."

Landis said, "How in blazes *did* she get out of there? Eilers had his own key, but she never came into the hall!"

Campbell turned from Eilers, to face the front of the room. "Some things are answered, George, by the only thing that could possibly have happened. This is one of them. She went out the window. It was the only possible way she could go without your seeing her."

"But she couldn't have jumped without breaking a leg, or maybe her neck," Martin Quest protested. His sleep-thickened voice was beginning to clear.

Campbell said, "No. Somebody put up a ladder for her. Again, it's the only way she could have gotten down with her bones intact. And none of her bones is broken. She was in such a panic to get away from here, to get back to the safety of her apartment, that she didn't have much sense left. I didn't think she was desperate enough to try anything like that. I thought she realized she was in absolutely no danger as long as she obeyed me."

Eilers said, "She was so sure somebody'd get to her and kill her before the will was read, she couldn't trust even you and me to protect her."

Ranny Overholt said, "But how could anybody get out to bring a ladder for her? All our doors were locked, and Landis was patrolling the hall every minute."

Campbell said, "Again, the only possible answer has to be the right one. Bess appealed to somebody on the sly to help her get away, never dreaming that she was making her appeal to the very person who was sitting around waiting for a chance to kill her . . . The killer was fairly desperate, too, you know. He'd killed Wark Andross, he'd killed Naomi. You all realize by now that Naomi is dead."

Sally Mace said, trying to repress a shiver, "But why would he want to kill your secretary?"

"She wasn't my secretary. You may as well know now, those of you who don't already know it, that Wark Andross had an older daughter by a former marriage. He had commissioned me to find her. I did not find her until after he was dead. She came to this house under an assumed name for her own protection. Her real name, Mary Elizabeth Andross."

Jewell Northrup said, "Oh, the poor little thing. And now she's dead, too. Strangled. How horrible!"

Campbell looked at her sharply. "How did you know she was strangled, Mrs. Northrup?"

Jewell was momentarily confused. "Why, I—I heard you and Thibault talking; your rooms are right across the hall from ours and the talk woke me up. You weren't keeping your voices down, and I guess your door must have been open. Thibault said something about somebody looking awful, and you said that strangled people usually do. I didn't think it meant anything, I went right back to sleep. But now, I just remembered it, and I suppose I simply jumped to conclusions."

Campbell said, "Well, you're correct. She was strangled."

Ranny Overholt said, "You haven't told us yet how anybody could get out to fetch a ladder to help her to the ground."

Campbell said, "The only way he could have gotten out was by a window. The beds are all fitted with stout linen sheets. Our murderer promised Bess to help her get away. He told her to watch for him, and when she saw him below to knock Eilers out. He took the sheet off his bed, tore it into wide strips and made himself a rough ladder. He fastened the ladder to something, went down to the ground. He went to the garden house, smashed the lock or broke in a window, took a ladder to Bess' window and helped her down."

Quest was watching Campbell steadily, his ugly face bleak. "You say *he* all the time. You're sure your murderer is a man?"

The detective said blandly, "It's a little awkward to say he or she all the time. Let's leave it at that, Mart. Our murderer choked Bess with a strip off the sheet, and left her dying on the patio flagstones. He returned the ladder to the garden house, climbed back to his room via his sheet ladder and pulled it up after him. He wouldn't leave those strips lying around. I think he cut them into short pieces and flushed them down the drain. I'm sorry to have hailed you all out of bed, but it's the first chance I've had to get him against the wall. I had to act now, and corner him before he could cover his tracks."

Francie Dunham had started to cry. Sally Mace put an arm

around her, and Jewell Northrup said, "Hush, Francie! Hush!"

The detective was looking at Francie Dunham. He said, "What were you doing in Naomi's room when I knocked at the door and asked if anything was keeping her awake, Francie?" The girl gasped, and sat stiffly upright, staring at him. Campbell went on relentlessly, "Why didn't you simply say it was you? Why did you imitate Naomi's voice and say you were just thinking?"

"I wasn't in there!" Francie denied, her voice shaking. "I wasn't in there at all!"

"There's no use in talking that way," Campbell said. "We know you were in the room. We know by your fingerprints—on the doorknob. You were there but you had left the room by the time I last tried the door to see whether it was locked. What were you doing there?"

Francie started to cry again. "I only wanted to speak to Nomy. And she wasn't there. I waited around a few minutes, and then I concluded she was gone."

"Where? Why?"

"She told me that afternoon she was about ready to chuck the whole business, sneak back to Beverly Hills and let you and Drake Freedon sweat out the fool will reading. I thought she'd done it."

"Why didn't you tell me so?"

"I didn't want you sending anybody to bring her back. I wanted her to get a head start before anybody knew she'd lit out. So I imitated her voice, to make you think she was still there. Then when you went into your own room, I just turned out Naomi's lights and ducked fast."

"What was the idea of locking Naomi's door?"

"Well, I didn't know you were locking everybody in. I

didn't know you had any keys. Naomi's key was in the door. I just locked the door and took the key with me, so you couldn't open the door and look in and see she wasn't there. And then after I learned she'd been hurt, I was sure she was dead and you were trying to trap somebody. I wouldn't say anything for fear you'd think I had something to do with it. And I didn't kill her. I didn't!"

"The rod that did kill her is in the brass tube over your bathroom window, Francie."

"I didn't put it there! I didn't! I don't know anything about it. You can't prove I had anything to do with it."

Campbell said, "Don't get hysterical, Francie. I know you didn't kill her. That had me puzzled for a while, thinking the same person had pretended to be Naomi after calling her out and killing her. When I considered the idea of there being two persons involved, the puzzle cleared up."

Francie slumped into Sally's arms, sobbing. "I loved Nomy. I wouldn't have hurt her for the world."

"Pull yourself together, Francie," the detective said quietly. He looked steadily at Martin Quest. "Our murderer is a man. I've known that all the time. I didn't want to state it flatly till I'd jarred Francie into telling the truth. I have known all the time that he had to be one of three men."

Quest said harshly, "What three?"

"Quentin Ireland, Ranny Overholt, or you, Mart—the three men who were with Wark Andross by the swimming pool that night. That gate locks itself. The key was on the inside of the gate. No one else could possibly have gotten into the enclosure. Don't anybody try to make a move. Eilers has a gun. Landis has a gun. I have a gun." The detective turned his head to glance at Thibault. "Thibault, go upstairs and see if there isn't a sheet gone off Martin Quest's bed."

Thibault whirled and vanished up the stairs.

Quest sat gripping the edge of his chair, his skin drained of color, his drawn lips baring his crooked teeth.

The faint thud of Thibault's feet running down the hall on the upper floor came clearly to the stilled living room.

Campbell went on evenly, "The motive was money, of course. Seven million dollars' worth of money. If both the Andross girls were dead before the reading of the will, it all went to Martin Quest."

Ike Northrup exploded. "Hell! Is that what the row was about?"

"That was it, Ike. That one paragraph in Wark's will."

"But Mart was trying to get him to change something!" Northrup looked at Quest with unbelieving eyes.

Thibault came rushing down the stairs to halt breathless in the doorway. "Yes, sir, Mr. Campbell. The top sheet is gone off Mr. Quest's bed, and the flush bowl is stopped up. That drain always did clog at the least excuse."

"Then it won't be hard to retrieve the evidence, if we need it," Campbell said. "Thanks, Thibault." He turned back to face the room. "You see what I meant. I had to move now—before our murderer had a chance to get another sheet from the supply closet, just as he intended to replace the rod he stole from the chair in Francie's bathroom, if Grannat hadn't obligingly done it for him."

Quest said hoarsely, "No. No, by God! It isn't true."

"It *is* true," Campbell said. "One man who pretended to go out of the enclosure that night didn't go. He slammed the gate to make Wark think he'd gone. Then he hid—probably in the bath house. He watched his chance to brain Wark. Then he did leave the enclosure.

"Tonight he turned on his radio to cover small noises. He

left it on till Landis ordered him to shut it off. By that time he'd disposed of the sheet and no doubt was ready for bed. But he wouldn't take the sheet off his own bed, Mart. He was trying to frame you. What did you kill Wark with, Ranny?"

Ranny Overholt sat bolt upright, stared around wildly, then leaped to his feet, made a rush for the door no more than five feet away, and sent Landis sprawling with a hard punch.

Campbell reached the other end of the room in a few long strides. Ranny was clawing futilely at the locked door. Campbell gripped him by the coat collar and slammed him back into his chair. "Sit there! Another move, and I'll chill you with a sock on the button!"

Landis got to his feet, scowling, hauling handcuffs out of his pocket. He said in a toneless chant, "I arrest you for the murders of Wark Andross and his two daughters. It is my duty to warn you that anything you say may be used against you."

Campbell's big hand was still holding Overholt helpless in the chair. Landis snapped the handcuffs over Overholt's wrists. The detective stepped back, and stood looking down at the man in the chair.

Ranny pulled himself erect where he sat, and glared up at the detective defiantly. "That's the wildest balderdash I ever heard. You can't prove a damned thing."

"Oh, yes I can, now," Campbell said. "There's the strip of sheet that was around Bess' throat. There's the stripped sheet in the drain. It's too bad the girl had to die to give us any real evidence against you, but you killed one too many when you laid hands on her. Till now, all I had was the fact that you were out of your room at the time Naomi was stabbed. I kept thinking the murderer was the same person who'd answered me from Naomi's room, and that had me stopped for a while since I knew you were in your own suite then. I'd locked you in myself. I knew you were one of the men in the enclosure the night Wark was killed, but reason pointed to Mart Quest as the murderer. He had the motive—a seven million dollar motive." Campbell looked at Francie. "Then it occurred to me that Francie could have gone across to Naomi's room while Sally was reading aloud to cover her absence. That's right, isn't it, Francie?"

Francie said wearily, "Yes. That's right. I didn't want you to know I was out of my room. I thought something was queer, having a detective in the house. I didn't want to get mixed up in anything."

Overholt said loudly, "You're still a mile off the track. I haven't killed anybody."

Campbell said, "Oh, yes you have. You've been tossing fish poles into cypress trees, too."

Ranny stared. "You're crazy. What would I do a thing like that for?"

Campbell said, "To get rid of it quick. No use denying it. Your fingerprints are on the fish pole."

Overholt looked at everybody but Quest, seeing all eyes on him, startled faces not knowing yet just what to believe. He said boldly, "Probably half the fish poles around the place have my fingerprints on them. What does that prove? What motive could I have for all this killing?"

"That's what has me stumped," Campbell admitted. "Unless you expected Mart to take care of you so you'd never have to work. And the more Mart had, the easier it would be for you."

Quest got out of his chair and came over to stand by Campbell. He looked tired and shocked, but his eyes were alert as he waited, listening.

Campbell went on, "My first definite lead toward Ranny came when I went to considerable pains to persuade you all that Naomi was still alive. It's always so easy to believe what we are afraid to believe, you know. All of you who were her friends, hearing she was hurt, were afraid that she was dead and I was lying for some obscure purpose of my own. Only the killer would be afraid that she was really living, and that his attempt to kill her had failed. All of you but one were at heart convinced that she was dead. Ranny alone accepted without question the idea that she still lived."

Ranny said derisively, "Nuts!"

The detective ignored him. "How did I know Ranny went downstairs for whisky? I had only your word for it, Mart. How did I know it wasn't Quest himself who went for whisky, killed Naomi, then told me it was the other way around to bring Ranny under suspicion, and cautioned Ranny not to mention it to me? All this time motive led to Mart Quest, as well as theory and indication. Did Ranny even know there was a Mary Andross? Did he know the terms of Mart Quest's inheritance? If he didn't know these things before, and if it were he who laid in wait in the bath house for a chance to kill Wark, then he must have heard Wark and Quest discussing them and learned about them then."

Quest asked flatly, "Are you through, Pat?"

Campbell shrugged. "I seem to be. I still have no reasonable motive for Ranny to commit all these murders, yet I know he did."

Quest drew his small, lithe body erect. He cleared his throat, and his voice rose, thin and hard. He bent his head and looked down at Ranny with no expression on his face. "I'll tell you what motive he had, Pat. I told you before, he's been like a kid brother to me, the only brother I ever had."

The detective said, "Yes. I remember. And I remember that Ike said at the breakfast table the only thing Ranny had any respect for was money—the lucre, Ike said. I knew either you or Ranny killed Wark. Ike was talking to Ireland after he came out of the enclosure, and they heard you and Wark still arguing. Ireland couldn't have got back in. But still, I was stumped. You had the money motive, not Ranny."

"You're wrong." Quest's hard gaze was still fastened on Ranny's defiant face. "I made a will. To whom would I leave what I had but to my kid brother? I left everything to Ranny. But Francie and I were—are to be married next month. After the wedding I would change my beneficiary to Francie, and he knew that."

Campbell pursed his lips in a low whistle. "That's a horse of another color! And if you'd been held for the crimes, sent to the gas chamber, he'd have wound up the sole possessor of the seven million." He was hammering away at Ranny, trying to break him down. Then he said the thing that did it. "You might as well give up stalling, Rann. Your fingerprints are on the rod Thibault found on the roof under Francie's window, too."

Overholt blinked, paling only a little. "They can't be! I took hold of it with a handker—" He caught himself a breath too late.

"One of your fingers must have slipped through the handkerchief," Campbell said. "You may get off with life if you come clean. If you prefer the gas chamber, that's your funeral."

Quest turned and walked away. He stopped and stood beside Landis, his back toward Ranny and Campbell.

Overholt slumped in his chair, limp, his florid face the color of old putty. He licked his lips. "What do you want to know?"

"What did you kill Wark with?"

"A rock. I hid it under the cypress trees."

"Cypress trees. Association maybe induced you to pitch the fish pole into the cypress tree below Francie's window; the place to hide incriminating evidence."

Overholt said, "It did. I even thought of it, after I'd shoved the rod Grannat had put up back against the wall with the fish pole."

"When did you put the sharpened rod into the tube over the window? When you and Mart stopped at Francie's room, and you asked to go to the john because your flush bowl was clogged?"

"That's when."

"Was the clogged bowl sheer invention? Or was it the truth? Thibault says that drain's tricky."

Overholt said, "It was just a lie to give me a chance to get in there and ditch the rod. But it's really clogged now with all those pieces of sheeting in it."

"When did you go in with the fish pole to poke the rod back against the wall below the window?"

"I don't know what time it was. The first chance I got when the girls were out of the room."

"Where'd you get the fish pole?"

Overholt suddenly laughed, derisively. "It's mine. It was in the closet in our room."

"How did you get into the garden house to get the ladder to help Bess down?" Campbell glanced behind him, to see Eilers sitting near, notebook open, pencil busy.

Overholt said, "I busted in a window. I had to wait for old Thibault to get out of the way. He was just leaving the garden house when I got there. And the absent-minded old fool went off with the padlock key in his pocket."

"He'd been putting the extension ladder away," Campbell

said, "after going up on the roof and getting the rod you ditched there. He already had brought the fish pole down out of the cypress tree. And I guess that covers that. We'll come down to bedtime, tonight. You got another sleeping pill down Quest that he didn't know about, didn't you? To make sure he'd stay sound asleep while you were moving about."

"Yes. In a drink of whisky. I hid the bottle on him, so I'd be sure to have some. He thought it was all gone, down my gullet. He was going to get another, then changed his mind for some reason."

Quest said without turning, "I *thought* I was damned dopey from just one little capsule."

Overholt said, "I opened the capsule, dumped the powder in the whisky, and flushed the capsule down the drain."

The detective said, "You freely admit that you killed Wark Andross, Naomi Andross, and the girl you knew as Bess Holloway?"

"Yes. I knew she was really Bess Andross. Mart told me."

Campbell turned to Eilers and said, "Got the confession ready, kid?"

"Right." Eilers rose and came forward, holding out the open notebook. He had written everything in longhand.

Campbell took book and pencil. "Sign it, Ranny." Overholt signed the confession without demur. Campbell glanced around the room. "Now all of you come up here and sign below him. He won't get far repudiating a confession signed by six witnesses. By the way, Ranny, when did you raise the sluice to empty the pool after Ransome had filled it?"

"Hell, I was sitting there in the cypress trees waiting for Ransome to get out of the way and go off to lunch. I went right in after him and yanked the gate up. I shut the sluice again after I killed Wark."

Campbell turned away. While the witnesses were signing, he stopped by the bell pull and rang for the butler.

Landis said, "I guess you're through with me, Pat?"

"Yes. I am, George. Take him away. Stop by Rupe Traid's place and tell him to come up here for the other body."

Landis unlocked the forward door of the living room, the locked door that had so efficiently stopped Overholt's attempted flight, tossed the keys to Eilers, and went out with his unresisting prisoner.

Campbell said to Quest, "Who bought off Doc Wheeler, Mart?"

"Why, no one bought him off, Pat. We put up a convincing story. He really believed it was an accident. Naomi was so wrought up and ready to go to pieces, he didn't even argue about taking Wark down to the undertaker's to keep a screeching ambulance off the hill."

"Thanks, Mart. I thought that probably was the answer."

Grannat's voice said, "You rang, sir?"

Everybody turned. The butler stood in the rear doorway of the room. A tall girl with chestnut hair and flashing eyes stood by him.

Campbell said, "The dirt's cleared out of the way, Grannat. The murderer is gone, in handcuffs, in Officer Landis' car. Will you introduce the lady, Grannat?"

The butler stood stiffly erect. "Yes, sir. Ladies and gentlemen, may I present Miss Mary Elizabeth Andross."

No one said a word. Quest walked slowly down the length of the room and stood looking her up and down. Then he smiled. "Well, by God! She is! She's a carbon copy of Wark— height, build and coloring. Welcome home, Mary!" He thrust out his small, finely formed hand. "I'm your second cousin, Mart Quest."

Mary Andross took the hand in hers with a warm grip. "Swell. I didn't know I was going to have any family left."

Quest whirled and half shouted. "Come up here, slow brains! Come up here and meet Mary!" He turned back to her. "This is Quent Ireland. Mary. Here's Francie Dunham, my fiancée, and her friend Sally Mace. And these two are Ike and Jewell Northrup, no relation to you, but Naomi's uncle and aunt on Sharon's side. Sharon was Naomi's mother, if you don't know, and she was Jewell's sister."

Jewell Northrup was excited and embarrassed. "Oh, dear. Things are moving so fast my head's swimming. I'm so glad to know you, my dear. I hope it won't be uncomfortable for you to have us around just till the will's read."

Mary smiled at her. "Don't be silly, Jewell. I'm going to need a lot of company for a long time. I'm tickled pink to meet the lot of you." She turned to Campbell. "But where's Bess?"

The detective said quietly, "Bess is dead. We'll go into that later at length, if you want to. Nobody's to blame but Bess herself. She ran right into it. Or should I call her Nina?"

"It doesn't matter. Her name *was* Bess, you know. Nina Bess Taylor. When she came to live with me, she dropped the Bess. And I always intended to drop it when I took my father's name." Her face was sober, her brown eyes dark. "And now she's dead. The poor, damned little fool. I tried to tell her, but she wouldn't listen."

Campbell said, "Don't let it get you down. After all, it might have been you lying out on the patio with a strip of sheeting about your neck, if she hadn't stood as your decoy."

Mary shook her head. "Not me, brother. I can take care of myself. When you were at the apartment that day, I wasn't sure I'd tipped you off, and I didn't dare put it any plainer.

She was right there behind the red portiere with that gun on me, the gun you took away from me tonight. She was so little she could hide behind a tin cup. It's a gun that used to belong to my stepfather. Just when did you tumble, anyway?"

The detective smiled. "Well, like Grannat, the instant I saw you, I knew who you had to be. You looked so much like Wark. And then, that picture of Wark as a young man, there on your bookcase."

"And when you called me up and asked if he was my father, you were letting me know you were wise to the set-up, and you were going to play it my way."

"That's right."

Eilers said, "Hell! I didn't need that to figure it out."

Mary turned to grin at him. "No? When did you figure it out, brother?"

Campbell said, "That's my assistant, Rick Eilers, Mary."

Eilers said, "I knew it was fishy from the first crack out of the box. She had herself all balled up. She lied and fell over in it."

"Such as what?"

"Oh, such as saying she herself quit school and went to work when she was fourteen or fifteen. I don't care whether she came from Arkansas, Podunk or Timbuktu; if she'd tried that, she'd know it couldn't be done. The laws of California say you have to go to school until you're seventeen. Even if you're graduated before that, you have to get a work permit from the truant officer of the school you attended. Her yarn was full of holes like that. It didn't make sense. But when I began to figure it with you as the real Mary Andross and her as Nina Taylor—with you taking after your old man and being a sucker for a hard luck story even if you didn't believe half of it—it made plenty sense. And when she began to howl that she wanted to go home, I knew. But Pat plays 'em close to his chest until he breaks a case, and I don't upset the apple cart."

Mary smiled at Campbell. "I see why you have him for an assistant. Or did he learn that kind of figuring from you?" Her smile half sobered, and she shook her head. "I can't help it—it hurts. To see her have to go that way. She didn't mean any harm."

Campbell said, "She threatened to kill you. That day in the apartment, if you'd given the show away, she'd have shot you, and you know it. She'd never get the money that way, but then neither would you."

Mary said, "She was only afraid I'd ditch her if I came into a lot of money and made a circle of new friends. I didn't have a day off till Saturday so I couldn't go to see you until then. She waited till I'd gone to work, pried open my tin-safe box, stole that sheet with the clippings on it and went to see you in my stead."

Eilers said, "But you knew damned well she wouldn't get away with it, didn't you?"

"Oh, I thought you might believe her at first," Mary said. "She was little and dark like my mother, she even resembled my father a shade when she smiled. She knew a good deal about me, but she didn't know everything. I felt sure she'd trip herself up sooner or later, yes. I knew the kind of yarn she'd spun when she fastened herself onto me in the park that day. I put her through high school, but it didn't do much good. She hadn't a brain in her head. She couldn't hold a job five minutes. My birth certificate was in that same tin box, but it wouldn't occur to her to look for that and take it along. The poor little dumb bunny, she'd just try to lie her way out of every hole that opened up in front of her."

Campbell said, "You *did* have your birth certificate then. You knew all along who your father was."

Mary's dark brows raised in surprise. "Why, of course. I had to have the certificate when I worked in the war plant cafeterias. Mother never made any secret of my real father, she'd given me his picture; taken when they were first married."

"I don't suppose you remember him at all?"

"Why wouldn't I? I was nearly seven years old, the last time I saw him, just before we left Seattle. He came one day to see me after Grannat had been gone only about an hour. I remember him distinctly. Mother never forgot him. She never stopped loving him. But she was hurt and bitter, at both him and Sharon."

"I can understand that."

"Yes, I can too, Pat. She brought me up to understand it. I used to look at his pictures in the paper, and wish I could know him. But I never would have gone contrary to her wishes for any consideration, not even after she was dead. She married again because she wanted me to have a father's influence. Ethan Holloway was a really swell guy, he was good to me, and I called him father to please him and took his name. But I always had a secret hankering to know my own father."

Campbell said, "He was as like you as two peas in a pod. He'd have done the same thing about Nina-Bess."

Mary looked at him. "She's upstairs, you said?"

"Yes. But you'd better not see her yet, Mary."

The girl said, "No. Strangled! No. I don't want to see her like that. I was so fond of her, the way you're always fond of anything that's dumb and dependent on you and helpless. I used to look at her homely little face and wistful eyes, and think of a cocker spaniel. I'll go on remembering her the way

I knew her, Pat." Mary turned, to glance at the butler, still standing in the doorway, brazenly listening. She smiled at him. "It's so good to see you again, Grannat! I think we could all stand a drink, don't you? You'll know what to bring."

Grannat beamed. "Yes, indeed, Miss Mary! I'll attend to it right away." He hesitated. "May I tell the rest of the staff, miss? They are all up. They know something has happened."

"Surest thing you know, Grannat. Tell them all. Tell them everything. Break out the larder and fill them up. Give them anything they want to eat or drink. I'll be in presently to say hello. I want to tell them we're all going to camp right here in the Canyon House till we die of old age."

Campbell thought, There's still the minor puzzle of Naomi's firing Ransome without her father's knowledge. No one would ever know why she did it. It didn't matter—it was of no consequence now. The detective's gaze lingered on Mary, on the beaming butler.

Grannat said, "It's wonderful to have you home, miss, if I may say so."

"Say any damn thing you please, brother," Mary answered, smiling. "You know me. Run along and fetch the drinks, Grannat."

Quest said, delight spreading over his ugly countenance, "Wark Andross, the second! I wish the old man were here."

The girl backed away, her lovely face somber, her brown eyes deep. She said to the detective, "Thanks for everything, Pat. Especially, thanks for being decent to her." Her gaze went over the faces of the waiting group. "You'll all excuse me, please? We'll have plenty of time to get acquainted later. Right now—I've changed my mind. I'm going up to see Bess. She's got that coming. I don't care how she looks. I'm the only one who loved her. No—don't come, Pat. I'll find her."

Campbell said, "It's the only door that's open, Mary."

She stood still for an instant, looking at the wall above the detective's head. "The only door that's open. That's what I was, you know, to her—the only door that was open. I'm not going to close it now."

She went out toward the stairs. The room she left behind her was as hushed as the room awaiting her at the head of the flight.

Campbell, recalling the words Quest had just spoken, thought, But—he is here. He thought, too, even for a man like Wark Andross, it was the best of all ways to live on.